D1295820

Rabbits, Crabs, Etc.

Rabbits, Crabs, Etc.

STORIES BY JAPANESE WOMEN

Translated by Phyllis Birnbaum

UNIVERSITY OF HAWAII PRESS
Honolulu

For Yoshida Yoshio

Copyright © 1982 by Phyllis Birnbaum
All Rights Reserved
Manufactured in the United States of America

"Fuji" originally appeared in Crosscurrents.

Library of Congress Cataloging in Publication Data
Main entry under title:

Rabbits, crabs, etc.

   Contents: Rabbits / Kanai Mieko — Fuji / Sono Ayako —
A bond for two lifetime-gleanings / Enchi Fumiko — [etc.]
   1. Japanese fiction—Women authors—Translations into
English.   2.   Japanese fiction—20th century—Translations
into English.   3.   English fiction—Translations from
Japanese.   I.   Birnbaum, Phyllis.   II.   Title.
PL782.E8R3   1982   895.6'3'00809287   82-8365
ISBN 0-8248-0777-4   AACR2
ISBN 0-8248-0817-7 (pbk.)

Contents

Preface

THIS collection must begin by remembering that the first eminent prose writers in Japanese were women. During the Heian period (794–1185), some exceedingly talented women of the court created literary works that still compel with the elegance of their style and the fine shadings of their insights. The eleventh-century *Tale of Genji* by Murasaki Shikibu is considered the world's first novel. Superb diaries and other prose works by women followed. Perhaps most significant among them was Sei Shōnagon's *Pillow Book* (ca. 1002), which sparkled with vivid descriptions of nature, court life, and sheer malice.

Historians generally point out that women writers in Japanese may have flourished during the Heian period because the literary men of the court were devoting themselves to now mostly forgotten writings in Chinese. It is interesting to speculate what turns Japanese literature might have taken had such women remained in ascendance. The rich variety of personalities and settings, the epic-length ambitions, not to mention Murasaki's respect for the conventions of plot seem far from the diffuse autobiographical novels which became the usual form in the modern fiction written by men.

In spite of this illustrious beginning, Japan's literary history since the Heian period is remarkably short on female names. With the increasing importance of the military class during the years immediately following, the influence of women in literature swiftly declined. Not until Higuchi Ichiyō (1872–1896) was another major female prose writer to achieve lasting fame. Gradually, as a result of the new freedoms brought by modernization, more women began to write and publish.

Again, scholars have brooded over the reason for these centuries of female silence. There is, however, simply no escaping the fact that Japanese women, genius and dolt alike, have for generation after generation been denied an average man's share of education, employment, independence, courage, confidence, self-respect, self-indulgence, adventure, orneriness, or anything else required to step forth from the house and into that difficult, exciting place called the world.

In this exclusion from influence and experience, women writers in Japan have not been an exception. Things are changing. These changes, however, generally seem as commonplace as an American automobile in the Ginza; it is still possible, in the latter half of the twentieth century, for a leading Japanese novelist to entertain an American female translator by urbanely pouring another cup of sake and assuring her that no, he would never dream of reading anything written by a woman.

In studying the women writers of the last century, one is often struck by the sheer oddness of their lives. Women were, apparently more often than men, obliged to abandon ordinary human comforts in order to write; there are too many stories of ostracism, wrecked marriages, and poverty in such women's biographies. Both talent and resilience were needed to establish themselves as writers.

Yet the very narrowness of their experience may have been turned into an advantage by some. Japanese literature has transformed detailed observation of single moments into passages of great beauty; the picaresque or journalistic novel has never appealed to the Japanese sensibility. Japanese writers often pause to feel the wind growing colder, the light sharper, or the moon shining more clearly through the maple leaves. Time stops in Japanese fiction while authors savor sensations and the reader, forced to stop as well, feels grateful for the introduction to moments that might otherwise be missed. Writing in such a tradition, women need not steel themselves to join revolutions or decapitate lions in order to satisfy the male arbiters of taste in the Japanese literary world.

Still, the modern women writers now coming forward will have enough opportunities for combat. The bookstores, demonstrating the maddening national fondness for categorization, relegate works by women to a special "women's literature" section. More ominously, critics of both sexes seem too certain about the capabilities of the female mind. "Her descriptive powers," begins one such brisk assessment, "are just like a man's in their thoroughness regarding light, color and smells, but . . ." And it is too infrequently that one finds a critical essay in a Japanese periodical comparing the woman's works under review to similar writings by a man.

The translations presented here are from works written in this century. The selections reflect my personal literary tastes and, although some well-known writers are included, I have not tried to present a comprehensive selection of writing by Japanese women. I apologize for the obvious omissions. If these stories demonstrate any notable trend, it is that society presses hard on Japanese women. The rooms feel too still and the air, old. Habits of daring are just starting to be learned. After short bursts of brazenness, the writers now seem to look around and ask for permission. Yet these writers are various in their longings for a good man, a son, solitude, even a taste of cruelty. They convey a sense of the world's unfairness by speaking for themselves rather than for the general condition of their sisters and in this they honor their art.

Acknowledgments

PROFESSOR Frank T. Motofuji of the University of California, Berkeley very kindly volunteered to check through the final version of these translations. For this and other extraordinary acts of assistance over the years, I am deeply grateful. A grant from the Translation Center at Columbia University helped to support my stay in Tokyo. My brother Stephen made sure I got there and back. Hamao Etsuko and John Nathan recommended some of the stories. Hara Toshiko and Takechi Manabu checked preliminary drafts. Back in Cambridge, I took advantage of Nancy Andrew's editorial advice.

These translations are dedicated to my friend who corrected my grammar and soothed my soul during a memorable year in Tokyo.

Rabbits

by Kanai Mieko

KANAI MIEKO (1947–   ) is the youngest writer in this collection and her promise has been noted by prominent critics. She mixes fierce intellectuality with playful borrowings from the world of popular culture. Her fictional experiments reflect international influences.

Kanai is also a poet and she relies upon a tireless visual sense. The descriptive passages in her writings are very specific, sometimes down to the product labels. This meticulously drawn reality contrasts with her dreamlike plots. In her early stories, her narrators wander through their days questioning the nature of their human relationships. Kanai has recently explored the mysteries of her own creativity. In the striking story "Platonic Love" (*Puraton-teki ren-ai*, 1975), the narrator, who is a writer, keeps receiving letters from an unknown person who claims that "the works published under your name were written by me." The narrator travels to a hot springs inn, where Japanese authors have traditionally gone to transcribe the voices of their muse. There she attempts to comprehend the source of her own inspiration.

"Rabbits" (*Usagi*, 1976) may be seen as another of Kanai's efforts to understand the puzzles of her imagination. She says that she decided to write the story after she had seen rabbit skins nailed to the door of a store and then had a dream in a train about rabbits. This narrator sets her mind loose on those images and no small part of the story's effect is her own surprise at the violent result.

When suddenly a White Rabbit with pink
eyes ran close by her.   *Lewis Carroll*

"WRITING (also not writing, since that is part of the
whole process) means putting pen to paper and this I can no
longer escape. To write would seem to be my fate . . ."

I wrote these words in my diary the day I pretty much
forced myself to go out for a walk near my new house. The doctor had been telling me how good a little exercise would be for
me and so, even though I'm not the sort who takes strolls will-
ingly, I felt obliged to follow his advice. Outside, it was all sky,
gray, threatening and looming over the landscape. Such weather did little to increase my interest in my health. But moving
myself seemed a far more pleasant alternative than sitting inside
and facing my diary, or all those pages of manuscript paper in
my depressing room, where the furniture still had to be put in
place.

I was anyway in quite a foul mood. Even when wide
awake, I felt as if I were in the midst of a bad dream. I lived in
dread of these gloomy days which would descend upon me always with no rhyme or reason. Something undefinable, something like an illusion—an odor, one might say, for want of a better word—followed me wherever I went; an odor like that of an
unseen bird that had flown right past my nose. I was aware of
something about the odor I could not quite put my finger on,
and was absolutely certain I had experienced that something.
But just as an odor drifts away and dissipates without form in
the air, so that elusive something would disappear. Then I would
feel vaguely deflated and upset, the same as when you're finally
able to read a message written in the sand at the same time that
a careless breeze comes along and sweeps it all away into a
wide, desolate stretch of gray.

With the smell, whose exact origin remained a puzzle,
came also a sense of nausea. I want to make clear though, that
the smell came from a place deep inside me and did not cause
the nausea, nor did the nausea lead me to the smell.

In the course of my walk, I lost my way and found myself in the garden of a vacant house in the midst of a grove of trees. Tired, I sat down on a rock and rested. Just then a big white rabbit ran by right in front of my eyes. By big, I don't mean big for a rabbit, since it was pretty much my size. But a rabbit without a doubt, nothing else could have had those big, long ears and, for that matter, the rest of its body also looked every bit like a rabbit. Springing up from the rock in an effort to pursue it, I was earnest in my chase until I suddenly fell down into a hole and blacked out. When I came to, the big rabbit was sitting quite close by and was staring at me.

"Who are you?"

"I was taking a walk and got lost and came here. Are you a rabbit? Or is there a more formal way you want me to address you?"

"I look just like one, don't I?" the rabbit said, making a happy chuckling noise down in its throat. "But actually, I am a human. Perhaps. These days, I really don't care what I am."

"It's amazing, you look just like a rabbit," I said, my voice full of wonder.

It was covered by a fluffy white fur coat, and when I observed the creature head on, I saw that it even had pink eyes. Upon further examination, of course, I could immediately make out that the eyes were glass lenses expertly attached to the rabbit mask and hood which it wore on its head. The white fur covering encased the whole body like those pajamas with built-in feet which babies wear. But why had this young girl gone to all this trouble to get herself up like a rabbit? She quickly sensed my question.

"You probably want to know why I go around like this, don't you? Well, I'll explain, though this is the first time I have spoken to anyone except myself since my father died. I absolutely must speak to someone. If I don't, I won't ever be able to calm down. So please, come in," she said, inviting me into her rundown house. The girl's name was Lily, which she didn't think particularly bad for a name, though Tiger Lily or Star Lily, she explained, would have pleased her more.

"But of course, no one knows my name now and there is no one around who remembers it. So I wonder if you would do me the favor of calling me Star Lily."

I have no alternative but to say that the interior of the house was a rabbit hutch. The floor had a wall-to-wall carpet of rabbit fur and on the walls were nailed fresh rabbit pelts with the limbs spread out to make the shape of an X. Pervading the interior was a strange animal smell. Even after I had sat down on the rabbit fur floor, the vile smell made my stomach turn over. The girl appeared unperturbed about my discomfort and kept moving her ears or scratching the back of her ear with her hind leg. Not that she particularly itched there, rather she had done this so many times that by now the reflex rabbit gesture was no doubt second nature to her.

"I have been wracking my brains for some time. There must be a logical reason why I have ended up like this. But I never could quite figure it out. The first inkling of what would happen to me occurred, I think, on that morning," she said slowly, as if trying to get her recollections in order.

"In the morning, I woke up and walked around the house, but no one was there. I looked in the kitchen, dining room, living room, bedrooms, closets, bathroom, toilet, and just to make sure, I opened the wardrobe and searched there, but couldn't find anyone. In the kitchen, the milk had been left on the stove with the gas on and the boiling white cream overflowed like meringue from the pot. In the bathroom, there was still soap lather in the cup which my brother used to shave with. In the dining room, the cup of chilled orange juice, apparently just taken out of the refrigerator, still had droplets of condensation along the surface. Also, the newspaper looked as if it had been left on the table by someone who had gotten up for a moment while reading it.

"In spite of this, there was no one in the house. I turned off the gas under the milk, drank the orange juice on the table, and while I was reading the paper (that is, I merely passed my eyes over the news items and didn't really read the news about the great happenings announced in large print. In any case, the news, either of foreign wars or the assassination of foreign prime ministers or foreign revolutions, had no connection with my life), I thought that they would not return; and were they never to return, I did not care at all, nor did I try and figure out why they had gone off. As a matter of fact, my family did not come home after that. Even if they had returned, I would have looked at them and almost certainly would have denied knowing who ❧ they were.

"It is possible that the attitude I took in regard to my family's sudden disappearance was strange, because I wasn't a bit surprised. Every morning, I had drunk a glass of orange juice while the rest of the family sat at the table offering each other opinions about the weather and the relative viscosity of the orange juice. I would eat my breakfast of toast and bacon and eggs and tea while my father gave a running commentary on the newspaper items. Only when my father asked me about my progress at school did I speak.

'What are you studying at school now?' was one of his usual questions.

'Oh, this and that. Physics, chemistry, and math.'

"Our conversations would end there. Smacking his lips and cleaning the egg yolk from the plate with a piece of bread, my father would mutter meaningless phrases. 'What you study now will serve you well in the future,' or 'No matter how old people get, they should always have a thirst for knowledge,' or 'There is no easy path to learning,' he would say, sipping his tea from his large cup. My father remained perfectly oblivious to the bits of yolk and drops of tea which had stuck to his curly mustache. Greedily downing his second helping of bacon and eggs and toast, he would repeat the same things over and over in his loud voice. (My father always spoke in a loud voice and even when he thought he was speaking softly, it always came out as if he were shouting at everyone.) I can hear that booming voice of my father saying,

'Eating a filling meal is sure to make you want to go happily off to sleep. At least any healthy person would feel this way.

There is no doubt in my mind that, physiologically speaking, this is perfectly healthy and natural. Yet, the world makes us go out and work. After eating breakfast, I feel like taking a little nap for an hour or two. I feel that way after each of my meals.'

"There was no response since everyone took what my father said with some measure of scorn. To the family, my father was a ruddy-faced pig who did nothing but stuff himself and sleep. But I was different. Of them all, I loved my father best, his panting after the sweet, lovely pleasures of overeating and sleep, and the undulating of his fat stomach. At dinner, I sometimes kept my father company eating dishes which the other members of my family would not touch until I was full and could hardly keep my eyes open. We would both burp unashamedly afterwards. When we were so full that we could not eat any more, we did not stick our fingers down our throats in the barbaric manner of the Roman aristocrats, but drank a laxative made from special medicinal plants. Then, totally refreshed, we would commence eating again.

"My father raised rabbits for cooking and twice a month, on the first and the fifteenth, he would kill a rabbit and prepare a dish. On the first and the fifteenth, he got up long before breakfast and selected a big fat rabbit from the shed and killed it. The rabbit, who had no idea what was happening, drew up its legs and just waited there with its ears firmly clutched in my father's hairy fat fingers. In its coat of fluffy soft white fur, the animal drew itself in rigidly and got strangled by my father's huge hands. Again and again, from my second-floor bedroom, I had peered down at a dead animal, placed on the ground in front of the shed, its feet sprawled out, its neck broken. After that, my father, working in the garden storage shed, slashed open the rabbit's neck, severed the arteries, and hung it upside down. While the blood drained out completely, my father would slowly eat a bigger breakfast than usual.

"After breakfast, my father would slit open the rabbit's belly and remove the innards. Putting the carcass in a wooden bucket totally brown from all the leftover blood, my father would skillfully set about stripping off the skin. When my father's thick bloody fingers moved, pink flesh encased with blood and fat came into view beneath the pure white fur. When the rabbit was neatly skinned, the corpse was hung from a nail on the wall of the shed. The fur, now completely clean of blood, was stretched out and nailed to the wall of the shed with its limbs spread out in the shape of an X.

"In the evening, when my father came home from work, he would prepare a meal of the rabbit in the storage shed. He stuffed the rabbit's belly with a liver, kidney, and raw sausage stuffing, and after adding onions, mushrooms, tomatoes, and various spices, he would simmer it. Sometimes he made stew, but my father and I both preferred spiced stuffed rabbit.

"To a certain extent, the rest of the family could accept having the rabbits around as adorable little pets, but they took a high-and-mighty attitude about using the fur or eating the meat. Moreover, they could not bear the thought of killing a pet just so that we could make a gourmet meal from it. They always said they hated the idea of strangling a small defenseless creature to death. It was despicable and shameful, they said, to then prepare the animal for skinning. As if that were not enough, the mere sight of us consuming the rabbits was an abomination that made them sick to their stomachs. My mother had no choice but to watch all these goings-on in silence (she perhaps thought she was better off than if my father had kept a mistress and thus wrought havoc upon the household), but she was absolutely opposed to making the rabbit dinner in her kitchen.

'Do you really expect me to stand by while you smell up the whole kitchen and house with rabbits? No decent household I know of reeks of animal blood and mine certainly won't be the first.'

"For these reasons, my father and I ate the twice-monthly supper on the small table in the storage shed. Beautifully browned, fat glistening, and legs still attached, the rabbit was placed on a large oval platter with a blue design of climbing roses. We used a dense assortment of limp tomatoes, onions, and mushrooms to garnish the rabbit. The shed was permeated with the voluptuous odors of cooking vapors, spices, and rabbit's blood, and the jovial air was like that at a banquet of knights in the feudal age.

"We also stuffed pigeons (which my father raised as well) with liver pâté and wild grapes, made a wrapping of grape leaves, poured on a bit of kirsch, and then roasted them. There was a pâté in aspic made from the innards and topped with sour cream as well as raw flat clams, round clams, and surf clams sprinkled with lemon, an assortment of chilled fruits in a compote, red and white wine, and ice cream with whipped cream and almonds. The climax of our dessert course demonstrated the heights of our gluttony, for we drank quantities of cocoa with Jamaica rum. During the whole extended period while we were cooking and eating, we did not attempt to make scintillating conversation. We concentrated only on our eating. Occasionally, we spoke to each other. My father usually asked me about my relationships with other people.

'What's happening? Do you have a boyfriend? Did you meet any nice boys at school?' he would ask timidly in his booming voice.

'School is hardly the place,' I would answer laughing. 'Father, your mind's wandering. There are only girls at my school. It would be pretty hard for me to meet any boys there.'

'Oh, that's right. I completely forgot about that. You really have no boyfriend?'

'No. I'm not interested in boys. I don't like those young kids. Just let one come close to me, and I'll take a bite out of him.'

'But sometime, someplace, you'll meet a boy. Then you'll abandon me and go off with him somewhere. That's for sure.'

"We had this kind of conversation over and over again. When we drank our last cocoa with rum, we were both full and very sleepy. My father would smoke a cigar, and while I took the time to slowly savor the taste of the cocoa and rum which was spreading along my tongue, I felt completely satisfied and sleeping seemed a pleasant idea. As I cut across the garden from the storage shed and returned to the house, the slightly cool outside air which brushed against me all the way up to the second-floor bedroom felt wonderful and made the prospect of sleep even more enjoyable. In the shed, the rabbits were all quietly asleep. From their coops, I could hear the pigeons' low voices, which sounded as if they were clearing their throats. The sweet smell of the flowers gently inflated the air.

'Good night,' my father said in a sleepy voice in front of his bedroom. 'Now off I go gently to my death, eh?' It was his usual joke.

"Then I remembered that this day was the fifteenth—to be more precise, I read the date in the newspaper—and I thought that my father must be in the storage shed making his usual preparations. But I didn't know what had happened to the rest of the family. I couldn't believe that any of them would have gone out to the storage shed to have a look at the bloody work they despised so much. But I couldn't imagine that they had gone any other place either. I settled on the thought that they had been spirited off somewhere and would not show up again, which was fine with me. Repeatedly, I had the feeling that we had been waiting for this to happen for a long, long time.

"After I drank up all the orange juice, I remembered that there was no one to make breakfast and I thought that I should prepare the meal for my father and me. I made ham and eggs, tea with milk, and toast. I wanted to cook something like the ceremonial red rice which would be appropriate for a special breakfast, and the color, I realized, would be crucial to the analogy. We would have to eat something red. There were radishes and strawberries in the refrigerator and I used those to decorate the table. I was delighted since I knew my father would immediately understand what the radishes and strawberries stood for.

"Still wearing the huge bloodstained apron which he used for preparing the rabbits, my father came in through the kitchen door and spoke, laughing and in the very best of spirits,

'Let's have breakfast. From this morning meal, let's make special dishes for each meal. You might as well stay home from school. A female student whose family suddenly disappears without leaving a trace is expected to stay home from school since she is beside herself with worry.'

'So they've really gone off, have they?' I said, growing more and more joyful.

"With my father's entrance, a warm animal smell had begun to drift about the kitchen and I inhaled deeply of that smell, thinking that from now on the house would always carry this aroma. From that time on, my father and I were absolutely happy. Every day, we made a different specialty, ate until we were full, and then slept. To our heart's content and without anybody ruining our mood, we experienced what my father always used to describe at every meal, that is, how natural and sweetly pleasant it was to sleep after eating.

"I stopped going to school altogether and my father left his work at the office for others to do. Since all he did was eat and sleep, he got fatter and fatter and occasionally would collapse with heart spasms. Even so, we never called for medical help, and when I did try to phone the doctor, my father got furious with me. All I could do was hold my tongue and obey my father. He had become so fat that when he sat down on the dining table chair, it made groaning noises as if it were about to collapse. The slightest exertion caused him to get out of breath, and he panted noisily like a train engine starting up. So before I knew what was happening, the job of killing and cooking the rabbits became mine. I developed a knack for this right away and set about my task with great gusto.

"At first I was a bit disgusted by the job, but soon I came to understand that even killing was one of the pleasures of life and I was happy when I stuck my hand into the still-warm belly of the rabbit and drew out the insides. So absorbed was I in my work that I felt I was plunging my hand into sweet roses of flesh. When the palpitations of the beating little heart were transmitted through the tips of my fingers, my heart also beat wildly. Of course, when I held the rabbit and squeezed its neck, I felt a pleasure that differed from that when I plunged my hand into its innards. To intensify the moment, I squeezed the neck trying various techniques. The rabbit was submissive as I held it up by its ears, and I felt the cruelty of killing this chubby soft white creature with my own hands. But I discovered that, by degrees,

my reluctance had changed into a sensuous pleasure replete
with a sweet rapture. Because the struggling rabbit would kick
and hit me in the stomach when I slowly tightened my grip
around its neck, my excitement rose to a fever pitch. Soon my
fingers could sense that they had broken the rabbit's neck. At
the same time, I would feel against my stomach the violent
spasm that wracked the rabbit's body from one end to the other.

"At first, I would lay the rabbit on my knees and strangle it
there, but I also tried killing it by putting it under my arm and
squeezing hard at the neck in a sidearm style. This technique
felt moderately good to me, but if I got a bit careless, the rabbit
would escape by slipping out from under my arm, so I didn't
have much success with this method. In the end, the technique
that gave me the greatest satisfaction was to strangle the rabbit
while I squeezed it between my thighs. I rather liked this method and continued to use it for some time. Then I got the idea
that direct contact with the rabbit's fur on my bare legs would
feel even better, so I changed from the blue jeans I always wore
when killing and started wearing a skirt. I pulled up my skirt
and placed the rabbit between my bare thighs. It did not take
long for me to begin performing the mysterious rite of the
bloody rabbit slaughter completely naked.

"Ever since my father took to bed almost continuously, I
killed rabbits for the mere joy of it, not only on the days when
we were going to eat them. A pleasure suffused with cruelty
makes you greedy for more, and this greed called for more
blood from the sacrificial rabbits but would not be satisfied.
Next I decided to bathe myself in rabbit blood while the animal
was hanging upside down and the blood was dripping out of it.
One rabbit's blood would not suffice to bathe my whole body. I
would need three or four of them. Using both hands, I did a
careful job of rubbing the blood all over my body. Once well
soaked with blood, I especially liked to arrange my pubic hair
neatly. I also enjoyed twisting my neck around and lapping up
the blood from my shoulders, chest, and legs with my tongue.

"Ultimately, I stitched together pieces of rabbit fur and
lived in a rabbit costume with long ears attached to a hood and

a rabbit's mask. The hood was especially well made. For the inner section of the ear, I used a bit of pink satin, with wire and thread to hold it up inside. A length of thick knitting yarn went from the ear section down through the neck and arm of the costume and could be pulled by a ring attached to the fingers of my left and right hands. The same arrangement worked for the tail, which moved when I pulled the string tied to my fingertips. Since I had mittens made of the rabbit's fur on my hands, no one could tell from the outside that there were rings on my fingers attached to the string. When I moved my fingers in the mittens, the ears moved freely—straight up or lying flat on the back of the head. In the same way, I could freely manipulate the tail.

"Of course, it took a long time to sew the rabbit costume together. The untanned skin was encrusted with smooth and very hard red, brown, and violet matter. But I felt that if I tanned the skin, I would not get the real feel of a rabbit, so first I bathed in rabbit blood and with my naked body still wet, I got completely into the rabbit fur and went jumping about rabbit-style.

"At about this time, when I had come this far in my quest for rabbithood, my father would mostly only thrust his bloated blue-black face and hands out from the sheets and simply lie there, absolutely still. To be sure, when he was in a good mood, he got up and we did things together. I took care of my father every day, but I had no desire anymore to have him examined by the doctor. In any case, both my father and I were adamantly opposed to having an outsider enter the house. Because I didn't know when my father would have an attack, I had to stay at his side as much as possible.

"At that time the house was absolutely full of rabbits, and in every room rabbit dung and rabbit fodder made a mess of things. I no longer had to make the trip all the way out to the storage shed in the garden to entertain myself. Even when my father had his attacks, all I could do was give him some water. I had no other choice but to wait patiently for the seizures to subside. And both my father and I knew that the final fit would end with his death.

"Then the time finally came for my father to be released from his attacks. Each time my father had one, he really seemed to be in agony and I felt I was going to die just looking at him. Since the rabbit costume I had stitched together so assiduously was all finished, I intended to put it on and show it to my father. I wanted to give him some fun and thought he would surely enjoy seeing me. I carried a placard which said, 'Stuff me and eat me please,' and I tied a big pink ribbon around my neck like an Easter bunny. That day was my father's birthday and I was excited at the happy thought of giving myself to him as a birthday present.

"When I put on the rabbit fur and went into the room (I had thoroughly rehearsed my imitation of a rabbit's jump and gestures), my father was so surprised that he cried out. I had thought that his surprise would immediately turn to amusement and he would set about using the rabbit, which was actually me, in our rabbit strangling ceremony. Of course, I would have to be properly submissive, but when my father would close his hands around my neck, and pretend to wring it, I would thrash about a little, and at the end, I would send my whole body into a spasm, finally going absolutely rigid and playing dead. After that would come the climax of the skinning ritual. Before putting my fur on, I had bathed my whole body in blood to make it look as if I were really a rabbit with its fur stripped off. It thrilled me to think of the moment when I would feel my father's hand groping around inside me. Unexpectedly, however, my father didn't realize it was me.

'Witch!' my father shouted. 'You witch, go back to where you belong.'

"I was so shocked that I couldn't move.

'Father,' I called out.

"My father grew more and more panicky, and, in a rasping voice, he kept shouting, 'Witch, witch!' and threw the cup and pitcher near his bed at me and everything else he could lay his hands on. The large enamelware pitcher struck me squarely in the face and broke the pink glass stuck in the eyepiece of the fur mask. I fell over and lost consciousness from the shock my whole face sustained and from the seering pain that shot from my face to the back of my head after the broken glass had pierced my left eye.

"A crimson darkness spread within my eye as if a flaming fire dragon had burst in. An incandescent blaze started to burn in my head and I plummetted into black depths. I don't know for how long I lost consciousness, but when I came to, I was still there, lying on the floor of my father's bedroom. My head and face, covered with the fur hood and mask, were completely soaked in blood. A fierce pain was making my face feverish. I got up slowly, but reeled badly and felt nauseated.

"With great difficulty, I walked over to the mirror against the wall to check my injuries. The pink glass had pierced my eyeball at an angle through the eyelid. The left eye seemed utterly destroyed. I took the hood and mask off my face and resolutely picked out the bit of glass that was stuck in my eye. There was such a lot of blood that I wondered whether the eyeball itself had not also come floating out. I looked exactly like a rabbit being drained of its blood.

"I took out a towel from a dresser drawer and put it on my left eye, tying it tightly behind my head. But I soon felt faint again and collapsed in front of the dresser. When I came to for the second time, I realized that my father had died in his bed. My father's face in death was, to put it simply, distorted with terror and hideously twisted. A face terrifying to behold, but not because it was the face of a dead man. It was the preservation of the magnitude of the horror which my father had felt before his final seizure that made the face so frightening. I base the deduction which follows on the way he had shouted 'You witch!' at me (he had, in other words, seen me as a rabbit), but my father must surely have thought that the dead souls of the rabbits he had killed had taken shape before him and the panic had hastened the onset of his last attack. Thus, you could say that I had murdered my own father.

"Every day since then I am haunted by the ghosts of the dead rabbits and have behaved like a large, one-eyed rabbit. In short, I have clearly confirmed that I can never again return to the world of human beings. Looking back on it, I see that I had lived like a normal human being until the fourteenth of that month several years back. Up to that time, I had been like any normal school girl and had kept hidden from my classmates

everything about my father's strange tastes—that he killed rabbits and cooked them. And I cannot say that I did not feel somewhat guilty about eating the cooked rabbits. If they had known
I had calmly eaten the rabbits I myself raised, my classmates
would have surely nicknamed me Tiger Lily. They were little
better than blind idiots—yes, I still call them this even though I
am blind now in one eye—and, just hearing the word 'kill'
would make the dull, vapid faces of those donkeys go pale. It
went against my nature to care about what people thought of
me, but a girl doesn't feel very good when she hears malicious
gossip spread about her. Of course, I am completely indifferent
to such things now and don't give a hill of beans about people's
approval . . .

"Yes. Now I am completely a rabbit. Lately, I have noticed
that my eyesight in my right eye is growing weaker and pretty
soon I'll probably lose my sight in that eye completely. When
your eyesight gets weaker, invisible things begin to be visible.
The power that makes invisible the things which you could see
and that makes visible invisible things develops naturally. I can
always see the face of my father in death. I can see that bloated
blue-black face with its eyes wide open, the nostrils flaring, and
him screaming. Especially when I am in the midst of strangling
a rabbit, his face will suddenly appear before me. Then my
hands grow limp and I can't go ahead with the strangling. It
was a terrible face. It was a terrible experience. Also the time
when I looked in the mirror and saw the sharp bit of pink glass
piercing my eye (the rabbit's eye had pierced mine) was quite
terrible, no doubt of that, but also beautiful. I never had been so
startlingly pretty as then—so pretty it sent shivers up my spine.
My hair was stuck to my head with blood. The ghastly wound
made by the shard of pink glass deeply imbedded in my left eye
sparkled brightly in the light of the lamp. What gorgeous make-
up it was! So struck was I that later, when I thought of that moment, the pleasure in killing the rabbits lessened.

"You probably have noticed this already, but the reason
that all the rabbits here have no eyes is because I have gouged
them all out. I do this because when I gouge out the rabbit's
eyes, which are like rose-colored glass with a filter of transpar-

ent red light, I can see clearly how startlingly beautiful I was
then."

I met her a second time long afterward. Just about the time
I had started to think that strange experience had all been a
dream (why? Because no matter how much I searched, I could
not find that rundown house in the midst of the grove of trees,
and no one knew about a house with lots of rabbits), I went out
for a walk one day and suddenly I had immediate recall of the
road. With an animal's homing instinct, I walked, following the
invisible smell or signal. Then I found the rundown house and
entered the room where I had talked with her. She had fallen
down in the middle of the room where white fur had been
spread wall to wall, and, coming closer, I saw a sharp piece of
pink glass stuck in her right eye. Much blood had collected on
the white fur beneath her head and a thin film had formed on
the surface of the blood. This thin film was glittering and rain-
bow colored, just like a membrane of gasoline on the top of a
puddle left on the road after a rainstorm.

This was the first time I had seen her unmasked face and I
can't say whether she was beautiful or not. There is no way to
describe the left eye except as a black hole hollowed out and
pulled awry. From the right eye, which had been pierced with
pink glass, the eyeball, hanging down by its muscle, had slipped
out, along with quantities of blood. The right eyeball had come
to rest like a pink pearl earring under a finely shaped transparent bluish ear. Contradicting my vulgar expectation (that it
would be like a rabbit's), the mouth arched into a beautiful
curve and was stained with the faded color of blood.

I peeled off the white rabbit's fur which had completely enveloped her body. Then I threw off what I had been wearing and
got into her costume. I put on the hood and mask which were by
her side, held my breath in the animal odor, and waited for a
long time crouching there without moving. A group of blind
rabbits gathered about us. She and I, along with the rabbits,
made no effort to stir and so we remained in that same spot, absolutely still.

Fuji

by Sono Ayako

SONO AYAKO (1931–   ) was one of the first women novelists to
emerge after the war. Articulate and unrepenting in their display of superior intellects, her women narrators seemed to proclaim the arrival
of the long-awaited postwar female. According to one critic, the Japanese word *saijo* (gifted woman) was revived in this period after long
disuse to describe Sono Ayako. In the story "Guests from a Distant
Place" *(Enrai no kyaku-tachi),* which was nominated for the Akutagawa Prize in 1954, the forthright female narrator considers members
of the U.S. Occupation forces whom she meets in the course of her job.
Her unflinching appraisal of the Americans in this story was striking
for the time. Aside from many works of fiction, particularly short stories, Sono has also written social criticism.

In "Fuji" (1975), Sono shifts her attention to a woman precisely
the opposite in temperament to the heroine she made famous with
"Guests from a Distant Place." The wife here is uneducated and excluded from the opportunities offered her ambitious husband. There is
a lifetime of wifely resignation in these few pages.

"Is Daddy coming home today?" asked her three-year-old son, Masayoshi, a kindergartener in the younger-age class, and Ona Tamiko answered,

"Yes, he'll be back on the afternoon train." Then she added, "When he comes home, you tell him all about kindergarten."

But as she said this, Tamiko was aware that her words lacked conviction. Her husband, Masami, worked for a prominent steel company. The oldest son in a household that consisted only of his mother and two other siblings, he had not been able to go to college. After completing high school, he had immediately taken the entrance examination for J Company and started to work at its Komatsu plant in Ishikawa prefecture. Tamiko had been working at the bank near J Company and eventually got acquainted with Masami.

They had been married for six years now. Since his youth, her husband had a built-in sense of being the head of a household. In Tamiko's eyes he was so firmly in control of himself that she could not believe there was only two years' difference in their ages. Tamiko used to spend almost all her salary from the bank on skiing trips. Masami was quite different; he sent money back home to his family in Noto and had carefully put aside enough to pay for their wedding ceremony at one of the company's recreational facilities. And although he had set his heart on taking their honeymoon way off in Kagoshima, he had, when his original plan proved impossible, settled quite rationally for a place more within their budget. They took a tour around the Kii Peninsula. Tamiko and her mother both admired Masami's self-control in the way he ordered his existence.

Masami and Tamiko gradually settled into married life in a tiny two-room apartment provided by the company at nominal rent. They made do with amusing examples of accommodation, covering a tea crate with vinyl cloth and using it for a television table. There were comical moments too, as when they found there was no room for a cushion that had been made from an old blanket, and they ostentatiously placed it on top of the shoe cabinet in the front hall. Nevertheless Tamiko was quite satisfied with the small pleasures which went into establishing her own household. And maybe the extra weight she put on proved how happy she was, as everyone said, although it was a matter of deep anguish to her when she could no longer fit into her clothes.

Shortly after their marriage Tamiko came to see Masami as not merely worldly-wise in his reactions to all that came his way, but also as rather unyielding in his way of thinking. It became apparent that Masami was taken aback when someone— anyone—knew something he did not. If some item of general knowledge was involved, that was understandable, but he was even embarrassed when he did not know the latest snippet of gossip about some entertainer or other.

"It really bothers me when Masami tells me in all seriousness that some actress is probably going to marry so and so," Tamiko grumbled to her mother. "Me, I know about those things because I read the gossip in the weekly magazines, but I've always felt it was totally trivial."

"But you shouldn't criticize him for his eagerness to know. These days a lot of people seem to think that not knowing anything is perfectly normal. When a person stops wanting to learn, that's the end."

Tamiko winced at her mother's words. She had almost no interest in learning. During her last class in high school, some of the students had cried, but Tamiko was so delighted she could barely control herself. All she could think was that this was the end of studying and tests and that she would be able to take it easy for the rest of her life.

Some wives were embarrassed that their husbands had gone no further than high school and even lied to the children about their father's education ("Papa is a college graduate, you know"), but Tamiko did not share those feelings at all. Since she herself hated studying, it didn't seem fair to expect much education in her husband.

When Masayoshi was born, Tamiko felt she was becoming too content for her own good. She was about ten kilograms heavier than she had been as a girl; but this meant that her breasts never ran dry. Even after she had weaned the baby, some milk, enough for a snack, still flowed. Every time Tamiko took a nap, the baby would take her breast, and both mother and child would sleep soundly, deeply content.

"Be careful you don't smother the baby with those breasts of yours," her mother had warned her, but the baby was clever enough to let go of the nipple when he went to sleep.

Around that time, her husband returned home one night with an intense look on his face.

"I wanted to tell you that I'm thinking about going to college. I've submitted an application," he said.

Tamiko looked at him vacantly, but quickly understood what he meant. J Company had a special employee training program which included a college-level curriculum. A worker with a good performance record (in lieu of his high school transcript) and a superior showing on the written entrance exam (in lieu of his college entrance exams) could enter the four-year program.

"I was going to consult with you first, but then I decided that it was my responsibility to make the decision."

"If you get accepted, you'll go to Fuji, won't you?" Tamiko had heard that the training institute was located near the foot of Mt. Fuji.

"Yes. If I make it, I'll only be able to come home once a month. For four years we'll just have to live apart. There won't be any change in my salary or in the company apartment here, so you don't have to worry about any of those things."

"I see. Well, whatever you think is best," Tamiko said, neither consenting nor opposing the plan.

Dimly, a thought had occurred to her at that moment, though she did not say so to her husband, "He'll probably fail, so it's not worth worrying about yet."

There were a great many applicants to the training center from each of the factories throughout Japan and achieving the honor and privilege of acceptance was no easy task. But Masami carried through on plans he set for himself. He was selected from a huge field of competing applicants and it was decided that he would go to Fuji. There was actually nothing to worry about. Only men lodged together at the training center. Perhaps some women worked in the office there, but the place was in the middle of an out-of-the-way mountain area, and the accommodations were just like a hotel.

Quiet and rather isolated, the center had a 10 P.M. curfew every day. There would be no time to go into town for drinking. He was not being paid a salary to fool around for four years, and he had been advised that only those employees who were willing to endure a monkish existence and apply themselves earnestly to their studies would be given the opportunity to enter the school. All the men accepted these conditions.

"I feel as if I am sending you away to get married," Tamiko had said two years before when she had seen her husband off.

Although he had claimed that he didn't need anything, she had bought him new pajamas and underwear. She also sent him the best bedding they had and a new small pan so he could fix instant noodles at night.

In enthusiastic letters, her husband would write:

"This school really has everything."

"Famous professors from many universities come and the foremost, top-notch technical people in the company give lectures. The lectures are not big, maybe ten in a class. It must be the best university in Japan."

"When I study, I can feel new knowledge seep into me like water sinking into sand. I can't believe that I could actually have lived this long without studying as I am now."

"Men must really be something special," Tamiko thought. As for herself, she could quite easily get through an entire lifetime without studying. Maybe reading the scandal sheets actually was one big waste of time, but she couldn't see what difference it made what she read as long as she read something. Even if she did not read anything, Tamiko did not feel herself at any disadvantage when it came to educating her child or helping out other people.

Her husband came home faithfully once a month. Masayoshi, having completely forgotten his father's face, had run away when Masami tried to hug him, but that quickly passed. Tamiko had some vague inklings that, little by little, her husband was turning into a different person. If someone had asked her what had changed in him, she would have had trouble answering. During their monthly meeting, which took on aspects of a tryst, her husband made ravenous demands on her. In that sense, the two days they spent together had a new, fresh sparkle to them.

But they had nothing to talk about. Tamiko spoke in great detail of all that had happened in her husband's absence, how Mrs. so-and-so had developed gallstones, or that some dog had gotten run over on the street in front, or that she had found a better place to grow parsley than last year's spot. Even before, Masami had not been exactly overjoyed to hear her relate all these stories, but after he had started living in Fuji, the look on his face showed clearly that her talk irritated him.

"Please stop talking about all that nonsense."

"Then what should I talk about?" Tamiko answered back, offended. "I can't make fancy conversation. I don't go to college like you do."

Her husband was silent but Tamiko felt deeply wounded. She accepted whatever life meted out to her. Her life might be foolish, but life was life.

In addition, her husband had only complaints about the inconvenience of their living accommodations.

"When I get up in the morning, the bathroom is freezing. I can't stand it," her husband said, having become accustomed to central heating. "At least you could put a hot-water heater in the kitchen and bathroom. In the morning, shaving with cold water, I feel so miserable."

"It's nothing to get excited about. There's always a kettle on the heater. Why don't you use that hot water?"

Today her husband was due to return home. The young Masayoshi was getting bigger day by day and had learned to wait for his father's arrival. But for Tamiko, the return of her husband was agony. She waited for him with a sense of obligation, just as he too was probably only coming home out of duty, she thought.

When her husband came home, he longed to eat Tamiko's pickles, although he never once told her directly how much he liked them. He ate a whole bowlful of her pickled cabbage, radishes, and turnips.

"Education does strange things to people," Tamiko muttered, carrying a basket and going out to get some pickles from the small cement-block shed in the back of their apartment. The cabbage and the radishes were all marinating to a natural amber color.

"What is this damn Fuji anyway," she muttered again. Before she knew it, tears welled up and fell into the pickling vat.

A Bond for Two Lifetimes— Gleanings

by Enchi Fumiko

ENCHI FUMIKO (1905–   ) began her career as a playwright, but is known principally for her works of prose fiction. She is the daughter of Ueda Kazutoshi, a classical scholar, and her writings resound with the glories of Japanese literary masterpieces. Thrusting the old mysteries against contemporary sorrows, Enchi creates an atmosphere notable for its eeriness. While the poetry of antiquity consoles and inspires Enchi's modern heroines, little other physical or emotional solace is to be found in this bleak female world. In such works as *The Waiting Years (Onnazaka*, 1949–57; trans. 1971), she bitterly dissects the sexual and spiritual deprivations of Japanese women. Enchi remains unpersuaded by romantic solutions and her women characters seem to stare, like the stark painting of a cat in "The Book of Cats" (*Neko no sōshi*, 1974), "eyes wide open, blurred, and gazing out into an unknown emptiness." She has also published a modern Japanese translation of *The Tale of Genji* (1972–3).

"A Bond for Two Lifetimes—Gleanings" (*Nisei no en shūi*, 1957) follows the two-layer fictional structure Enchi favors. The fragment from Ueda Akinari's *Tales of Spring Rain* floats within the spirit of a modern heroine and serves as commentary on her life. Akinari's tale spoofs the popular Buddhist belief that a priest could go into a lengthy trance and later emerge physically untouched by the ordeal. In this case, the "priest" who emerges from the trance is hardly the pious, awe-inspiring figure of Buddhist legend. The widow in this story reflects seriously upon the priest's reappearance because she still longs for her dead husband, who might also, by some miracle, return. For in her mind reverberates the old teaching that marriage is a bond that extends over two reincarnations. A sentence in this story, "My very womb cried out in longing," caused a stir when the work was published.

K NEELING down on my knees in the veranda, I called out through the faded, patched sliding door,

"Professor, is it all right if I come in?"

From within came his unclear, thick reply which could have been yes or no, and there was the muffled sound of his bed-clothes as he shifted position in bed. Since I knew this was his usual answer, I softly slid open the door and, still in my overcoat, I went in.

As I had anticipated, Professor Nunokawa had lifted his head, with its rumpled white hair, up from the rather dirty pillow and was just then groping for the large, thin revised edition of his book that lay at the side of the pallet. Every time I came to take notes for him, I noticed the dirty fuzziness of the coarse sheets and the strip of white fabric attached to the edge of the quilt. The maid, Mineko, who looked after the professor, seemed to let many days go by without changing the linen. Even a young person in a fetid sickbed would look quite miserable; an old man lying in such a state seemed even more appalling.

I didn't know when my feelings of pity or compassion had actually turned into an abhorrence of this wretchedness. Even as my abhorrence grew with each breath I took of the steamy mildewed smell of the sickroom, I inquired soothingly after the professor's health. Before she had gone out to shop, Mineko had evidently made preparations for my visit by drawing an old sandalwood desk, whose sheen had utterly vanished, close to the side of the bed. I spread my notebook out on the top of it.

The professor had a hot-water bottle in his bed. Since the few pieces of charcoal in the small china brazier were forever going out, the room became bitingly cold on days like today when the early winter rains occasionally mixed with snow. Following the suggestion the professor had made at our first session, I kept my coat on and sat through each meeting still dressed for the outdoors.

"Today we're going to do 'A Bond for Two Lifetimes,' aren't we?"

The professor didn't want to discuss his illness, and so he

lay face up and opened the thin book on his chest. He took a red pencil in his right hand and looked at me by moving only his eyes behind his thick-rimmed spectacles. On the desk, I opened the same revised version of *Tales of Spring Rain* that the professor held.

"Page fifty-nine is where 'A Bond for Two Lifetimes' begins," I said.

The professor was working on colloquial versions of Ueda Akinari's *Tales of Moonlight and Rain* and *Tales of Spring Rain*, which would become a volume in a series of Edo literary works put out by the publishing company I worked for. I had undertaken to act as secretary for Professor Nunokawa, my former teacher, as he dictated, since he was apparently unable to write for himself. Even though he was sick, he had worked up much enthusiasm for this colloquial translation because he needed the money.

I had already finished recording the colloquial version of the nine gothic tales from *Tales of Moonlight and Rain* and had completed the first five stories in *Tales of Spring Rain*, all dictated by the professor through lips, puckered in their toothlessness, which narrated the stories carefully and almost without hesitation like a silkworm spitting out thread. In *Tales of Spring Rain*, a work of Akinari's later years, the preface states:

"How many days has it been now that the rains of spring have brought this touching quiet? I picked up my usual writing brush and inkstone and thought over various matters but found I had nothing to write. Copying the old-fashioned storytelling styles is a job for the amateur writer, but I, living like a mountain rustic, have hardly any subjects to write about. I have been deceived into believing in the things people have described about the past and the present, and, thinking them true, have related these tales to others, thus deceiving them as well. In any case, there will be people who, as the tales are told, will continue to take these made-up stories as real situations. Yet I'll continue to tell tales while the rains of spring fall."

With these words in mind, the old author seemed to feel he had progressed beyond *Tales of Moonlight and Rain*, which had delicately spun novelistic details together, and now dismissed his old style of writing as "a job for the amateur writer." Nevertheless, he continued to record his dark, hidden, and uncontrollable passions freely, boldly, and without constraint, these being dramatized by historical personages, in folklore, and legends. There are many stories in *Tales of Spring Rain* which diverge from accepted feudal morality, so it was to be expected that the work did not become as popular as *Tales of Moonlight and Rain*, and not many copies were handed down through the generations.

In his later years, Akinari's old wife had died. He also had no children and the sight in his left eye had gone. For a considerable period of time, he lived in a faintly illumined world, troubled by problems of food and clothing and shelter. Professor Nunokawa had established a reputation as a scholar of Edo literature. His oldest son had died during the war and his wife had also passed away. His only daughter, who was married, hardly ever came to see him because of his uncompromising character and also because she hated the fact that Mineko was always around.

Without either pension or annuity, the professor could continue the revision of manuscripts and dictation only because he had the help of a mere two or three of his students in his old age. While he was translating *Tales of Moonlight and Rain*, I had not noticed as much, but by the time we got to *Tales of Spring Rain*, I was often struck by the similarity of Akinari's last years and the present life of Professor Nunokawa. There were times when the professor's dictation sounded as if it emanated quite spontaneously from an essential source within his own core. The professor stood the book on his chest and he began to speak gently in the low voice people use to commence recitations of Buddhist prayers.

"During one autumn in Yamashiro province, all the leaves had fallen from the tall zelkova trees. The strong chilly wind blew down over a mountain village. It was cold and exceedingly lonely. There was a rich landowner whose family had lived in Kosobe village for many years. They owned many mountain fields and lived in such comfort that the family did not worry nor make a commotion if the harvests were good or bad.

"Thus the head of the house quite naturally read books as his hobby and made no effort to seek friends among the village people. Every day, until late at night, he read books under his lamp. His mother would worry about this.

" 'Shouldn't you be going to bed soon? The temple bell has already struck twelve. Father always used to say that if you stay up late at night reading books, you will wear yourself out and end up ill. When people enjoy doing something, they tend to immerse themselves completely in their own entertainments without being aware of what is happening. Then they regret it later,' she said, offering him her views on the subject.

"He took her warning as a sign of motherly affection for him and, feeling grateful to her, resolved to be in bed after the clock struck ten. One night the rain fell gently, and in the stillness that had settled from early evening no other sound was heard. Consequently, he got so lost in his reading that much time passed without him realizing it. This night he forgot his mother's warning, and when he opened the window, thinking that it might be two o'clock in the morning, the rain had stopped, there was no wind and the late-night moon had risen in the middle sky.

" 'Ah, what a quiet night it is! I should write a poem about this moment,' he said, and, rubbing an inkstick over the inkslab, took up his writing brush. He put his mind to one or two poetic lines, and while inclining his head and trying to think of more, he happened to hear something like a bell ringing among the chirping of the insects, until then the only sounds. Strange, he said to himself, now that he thought about it, this was not the first time that he had heard the sound of this bell. He absorbed the odd realization that every night when he had been reading his books like this, he had heard that same noise. When he got up and went into the garden to have a look here and there to find the source of the sound of the bell, he went to the place he thought the noise had originated, beneath a stone in the corner of the garden where there was a clump of unmowed grasses. After making sure that this was where the sound was coming from, he returned to his bedroom.

"The next day he called his servants together and ordered them to dig beneath the stone. When they had dug down three feet, their shovels struck a large rock. After removing that rock, they saw something which resembled a coffin with a lid on it. Expending great effort, they lifted off the heavy lid, and when they looked inside, they found a peculiar object which now and then rang a bell it held in its hand.

"When the head of the house, followed by the servants, came close and nervously had a look, they saw a form which might have been a human being, and then again might not. Its appearance was parched and hard, shrivelled up like a dried-up salmon, and bony. The hair had grown long and hung down to the knees. The head of the house ordered a strong servant to pick the thing up and carefully bring it out of the coffin. The man exclaimed when he had picked up the body.

'It's light, very light, like nothing at all. Doesn't seem to have an old man's ripe smell,' he said loudly, half-frightened.

"Even when the people lifted the thing out, the hand kept on ringing the bell. The head of the house looked upon the object, and he reverently clasped his hands together and prayed, saying to the others:

'This is what is called "entering a trance," which is one of the ways priests die, as Buddhism teaches. While still alive, some priests sit down in their caskets and die while meditating. This is what must have happened to this person. Our family has been living in this place for over one hundred years, and since I have never heard anything about such an event, it must have occurred before our ancestors came here. Did his soul go to paradise and only his undecayed flesh remain here? And what tenacity, to have only his hand keep ringing the bell as before. Since we have dug him up, let's see if we can bring him back to life.'

"The head of the house helped the servants bring this thing, dried and hard like a wooden statue, into the house.

" 'Be careful! Don't bump against the post and smash it,' he said, as though they were carrying a breakable item. Finally it

was placed in one of the rooms, and carefully covered with
quilts. The head of the house filled a teacup with lukewarm water, came to the thing's side and pressed the liquid upon the
dried lips. Then, a black object like a tongue emerged sluggishly
and licked its lips and soon seemed to be sucking eagerly at the
cotton wad soaked in water. Upon seeing this, the women and
children raised their voices in terror, 'How horrifying, horrifying! It's a ghost!' and ran out, refusing to come near again. The
head of the house, encouraged by the changes in the thing,
treated the dried-up creature with care. His mother joined him
in giving it lukewarm water, each time remembering to utter a
Buddhist prayer. During the passage of about fifty days, the
face, hands, and legs, which had been like dried salmon, re-
gained their moisture bit by bit, and some body warmth seemed
to have been restored.

" 'Truly, he's coming back to life!' the head of the house said
and doubled his care and ministrations. As a result, the eyes
opened for the first time. He moved his eyes toward the light but
didn't seem to see clearly. When he was fed rice water and weak
porridge, he moved his tongue and seemed to taste. He seemed
to behave like an ordinary person whom you might find anywhere. The wrinkles on his skin, previously like the bark of an
old tree, stretched out and he put on more flesh. He could move
his arms and legs more freely. He seemed to be able to hear, for
when he became aware of the gusts of the north wind, his naked
body shivered as though he were chilled. When he was offered
some old padded clothes, he put out his hands to receive the offering with great pleasure. He also developed an appetite.

"At the beginning, when the head of the house had thought
of the man as the reincarnation of a revered personage, he had
treated him with respect and did not dream of giving him the
unholy flesh of fish to eat. When the new arrival, however, saw
the others partaking of fish, he licked his lips to indicate how
much he hungered for it. And when such foods were put upon
his tray the guest gnawed at the bones and ate every single bit
with great gusto. The head of the house felt his spirits sink.

"Then the master asked him politely, 'You have gone into a

trance once and it has been your unusual fate to return from the dead. To make this religious experience more inspiring to us, could you tell us about what it was like living for such a long time beneath the earth?'

"The man just shook his head and said, 'I know nothing,' and looked stupidly into the master's face.

" 'Even so, can you not at least remember what happened when you went into the ground? In your previous life, what name did they call you?'

"The man was thus questioned, but could recall nothing. He became bashful, moved back, sucked his finger and was no different from any doltish peasant farmer from the area.

"All his efforts of the past several months and his exaltation in the belief that he had restored some worthy cleric to life having come to nothing, the master was thoroughly disheartened by the turn of events. Afterwards, he treated the man like a servant and had him sweep the garden and sprinkle the water. Not seeming to mind in the least such menial work, he was not lazy as he went about his chores.

" 'Buddha's teachings are quite ridiculous. Where has all that piety gone which was supposed to be strong enough to put him in a trance, and sustain him there for over one hundred years buried in the earth, and cause him to tap his handbell? There's no trace of nobility in his character. What is it supposed to mean that only his body has come back to life?' the master of the house said and others in the village also joined him, knitting their brows in consternation."

"Let's stop there for now."

The professor had turned to rest on his side without my noticing it. He listlessly put down the book which he had been holding until then.

"You must be tired. Shall I bring you tea?"

"No," he said, pursing his lips sourly. "Has Mine come back? I must go to the bathroom. Could you call her for me?"

I got up very quickly and slid open the room divider. I called out in a high-pitched voice to Mineko, already back from her shopping and apparently somewhere in the kitchen.

"Mineko! Mineko! The professor has to urinate!"

The professor had problems with his bladder and urinated with difficulty. He usually used a catheter to relieve himself, but since there had been one time during his dictation when he had felt sudden discomfort and had ended by soiling himself, I became a bit frenzied.

The rumor was that the professor had nicknamed Mineko "Goddess of the Narrow Eyes,"* and when she—with her slits for eyes and flabby white flesh—came running in from the kitchen, I switched places with her and went into the adjoining family room. There Mineko seemed to have been working on her knitting, for the red sweater she was in the process of making lay on top of the dirty printed cotton brazier cover and had two or three knitting needles stuck in it. Since the room was cold, I surreptitiously slipped my hands under the brazier cover and, listening to what was taking place in the next room, guessed that Mineko had slid the urinal under the professor.

"There! Now a little more . . . Lift yourself up a bit more, that's it, now we're fine," she said, raising her voice as if issuing commands, and then she said bluntly, between gasps, "Professor, it's time you dismissed Mrs. Noritake, isn't it . . . Well isn't it . . . It's time you dismissed . . ."

"No. Not yet. We're just taking a break. You finish this up now."

"Take your time. I'm just organizing my notes," I called in.

The professor did not answer. The insertion of the narrow rubber tube must have been painful.

"Oh, that hurts." "Don't be so rough!" His carping voice came to my ears a number of times like moans, and no sooner did I realize that he had stopped scolding than I heard the thin trickle of urine splashing into the urinal through the tubing—a sound that expressed only too bleakly the meager store of the professor's life.

More than ten years had passed since I had graduated from

---

* Goddess who, according to ancient myth, performed a rousing dance, baring her body, to tempt the Sun Goddess from the cave where she had hidden and left the world in darkness.

my women's college. Professor Nunokawa, who was a teacher there, favored me a great deal by lending me books and having me help him with his research. During that time, with a boldness that astonished me, he would rub his body against mine, squeeze my hand and brazenly make advances suggesting further intimacies. Since I was engaged to my husband at the time —he was later killed in the war—and was just about to get married, I took the professor's advances as a middle-aged man's impudence. I found him altogether repugnant and sustained my contempt throughout our relationship.

I looked back on these incidents in the light of the scandals that had brewed in those days over the professor's lechery, which were so thoroughly unbecoming a teacher. I now realized that the energies of a man in the prime of his life must have been brimming over his body. The professor had nicknamed me Tamakazura, after the daughter of Prince Genji's great love, and at about that time, I myself lost my husband, barely a year after my marriage. He had been a technical officer in the navy and was killed in an air raid upon a military base in the homeland. I was a bereft war widow with a young boy to look after, living a marginal existence in the ten years since the end of the war.

As a woman alone, and working in those harsh postwar conditions, I encountered many bald advances from various men, of a sort even worse than Professor Nunokawa's. But I came to typify the proverb "A woman widowed in her twenties will be able to live forever without remarrying," because I felt both my mind and body fully, naturally moistened and blossoming from the mere year or more of contact with my husband. Whether for good or ill, I had passed these months and years without the opportunity of becoming attached to a second man. Now past thirty and holding down a job in a publishing house, I might appear to others to be a woman as parched in body and soul as the dried-up salmon in the story. But deep within my being, I sometimes embrace my husband in my dreams and I often feel the miracle of seeing my husband's visage quite vividly in the face of my small son.

As a result, I have recently begun to view the inevitable sexual aggressions of men with a sympathetic eye. When I realized that for the unprincipled Professor Nunokawa, who had in the past paid court to me tenaciously, life meant the putting of all his energies into producing a paltry quantity of urine in the next room, my whole being shook and I was brought very close to tears.

When I was called in again and entered the room, Mineko, disposing of the urinal, had vanished behind the sliding doors. It may have been my imagination, but the professor seemed to have more color in his face as he leaned upon one elbow on the pillow.

"What do you think of this story? It's interesting, isn't it?" the professor asked me, enthusiastically.

"Very much so. I didn't know that there was such an interesting story in *Tales of Spring Rain*. Was it taken from another source?"

"Naturally," he said and the learned professor spoke to me about "The Attachment Which Plagued the Trance," a story from *The Old Woman's Teatime Stories*, on which Akinari had apparently based his story. In 1653, a priest named Keitatsu of the Seikan Temple on Mt. Myotsu in Yamato-Kōriyama was about to go into his trance. Suddenly, he became infatuated with a beautiful woman visiting the temple and was unable to attain enlightenment. Fifty-five years later, still unable to subdue his own soul, he was beating his handbell and drum.

"The preface to *The Old Woman's Teatime Stories* dates from the early 1740's, probably written when Akinari was a child. In any case, since the work comes from that period, he wouldn't have been able to get a copy easily and so Akinari might have read it decades later. If Akinari had written this story in the same frame of mind as when he had written *Tales of Moonlight and Rain*, I think he might have described the part about the priest's infatuation with the beautiful woman in more detail."

As I listened to him say this, I lowered my eyes and thought that the professor might be expressing something of his own feelings here.

"Actually there's another story told about this. *A History of*

Fictional Biographies, written by Tsubouchi Shoyo and Mizu-
tani Futo in the Meiji period, relates the story of Aeba Koson,
who had heard about a man who had supposedly seen the manuscript version of Akinari's *A Tale of Rainy Nights*. According to
the story, *A Tale of Rainy Nights* resembled this "A Bond for Two
Lifetimes," but the ending is quite different. They are similar up
to the point where the bell sounds below the ground, but then
the story goes on to say that the man who hears the bell himself
digs a hole. There he finds an old Buddhist priest who had gone
into a trance and had been reciting sutras with fierce concentra-
tion. So the man brought the priest out above the ground, and
under the light of the moon, they opened their hearts to each
other and discussed many a matter. Even this format, religious
questions and answers, was quite possible for Akinari."

"But this version is more typical of Akinari, don't you
think, Professor?" I said, objecting.

The story of the fanatical faith of a priest who had gone
into a trance and wholeheartedly recited the sutras for decades,
but had still been unable to free himself from the mortal encum-
brances of skin and bones might have been pleasing irony for
the argumentative Akinari, since it showed how firm belief does
not necessarily bring the expected rewards. But for me, the latter part of the story which the professor was now translating
into colloquial Japanese had by far a more fulsome eeriness and
deep pathos.

"Ha, ha, ha," the professor laughed weakly, his sharp
Adam's apple twitching. "You want that to happen to you, don't
you? That's perfectly natural. You would like to have a bond
that extends over two lifetimes."

It was in the professor's nature, when he felt better, to utter
witticisms that were not exactly in good taste.

"I still have time. If you're not tired, shall we go to the end
of the story?" I said, edging up to the desk.

"Yes, let's try. If we can get through with this, we'll be able
to finish the rest easily."

The professor lay down on his back again and opened the
book on his chest.

"We did up to here, didn't we . . . 'Really, the teachings of

Buddhism serve no benefit. He entered the earth like this and rang his bell for over one hundred years. How fruitless that there is no trace of it and only the bones remain . . .'?"

"Yes, that's where we left off."

"Upon observing the dimwittedness of this man, the mother of the head of the house gradually changed her whole attitude toward life.

" 'For these many years, I have thought only of avoiding suffering in the world hereafter. I have been extraordinarily generous in my almsgiving and charity at the temple. Morning and evening, I never fail to utter a Buddhist prayer. When I look at this man here right in front of my eyes, I feel I have been duped by a sly fox or cunning badger,' she said and even told this to her son.

"Save for visiting the tombs of her parents and husband, she abandoned her religious duties. Not caring a bit for the opinions of her neighbors, she went off on moon-viewing picnics and when the cherry blossoms bloomed, and, taking along her daughter-in-law and her grandchildren, was concerned only with enjoying herself.

" 'I visit with my relatives often and pay more attention to the servants. Occasionally I give them things. I now live in peace and ease, having completely forgotten that I felt grateful for the chance to utter Buddhist prayers and listen to sermons,' the mother would say to people. As if loosed from chafing restraints, she behaved in quite a youthful, lively manner.

"Although the disinterred man was usually quite absentminded, he would get angry if he didn't get enough to eat or if someone scolded him. At these times, he would knit his brows and mutter complaints. The servants and the local people stopped treating him with even the slightest trace of reverence, and in his name alone, Jōsuke of the Trance, remained traces of the fact that he had entered into a trance and had come back to life. For five years, he remained as a servant in this house.

"In this village there was a poor widow. This woman was also regarded as rather stupid, and at some point she became intimate with Jōsuke of the Trance. He was seen diligently cultivating her tiny fields and washing the pots and kettles in the back stream. Since only circumstances had forced him to agree to employ Jōsuke and keep him for the rest of his life, his master, once this state of affairs became known, smiled wryly and, along with everyone else, actively encouraged Jōsuke to enter into an alliance with the woman, and Jōsuke finally became the woman's husband.

"Rumors flourished:

'He says he doesn't even know how old he is, but he seems to remember quite well how men and women behave together.'

'Very true. On the face of it, there seems to be a reason for Jōsuke's return to earth. Everyone thought he had been down in that hole ringing his bell morning and evening because of a pious wish for Buddha's providence. So, he actually was set upon coming back to our floating world of pleasure only to have sex, eh? What a noble desire that was!'

"The young people of the village went to great lengths to investigate how Jōsuke and the widow were carrying on. When they peeped in through the crevices of the wooden door of the dilapidated house, it was no monster they saw cavorting with a woman. They returned home dispirited.

'In spite of all the religious principles about cause and effect which Buddhism teaches, when we see such an example before our very eyes, all our faith vanishes.'

"This became the common talk among the people of the village. Almsgiving to the temples in Kosobe declined, and in the neighboring villages as well.

"The chief priest of the temple, whose family had enjoyed a prestigious position in the village for a long time, noticed these changed attitudes most. It is quite difficult for people living in this earthly world to fathom how Buddhist salvation, so beyond mortal imagination, is effected. But he could not condone the destruction of the belief in Buddhist virtues on account of the events taking place before his very eyes. He resolved to investigate when it was that Jōsuke had entered into his trance, and at least to resolve the terrible confusion in the minds of these foolish men and women.

"He consulted the temple's death registry and questioned every elder of the village. He made such efforts to find the buried truth about Jōsuke that he forgot to perform the required services at the temple. Unfortunately, after a big flood in the village over one hundred and fifty years ago, the houses and villagers had all been washed away. Moreover, a new branch in the river had emerged and the topography changed. After the irrigation facilities had improved, the people started living there once again.

"Thus, where the village was before the flood now corresponded to a place somewhere in the middle of the river. Since the region now called Kosobe was formerly at the sandy bank of the river where no houses had stood, it was impossible to discover why the coffin of the priest had been buried there.

" 'But if the holy saint had been trapped in the flood, water must have poured into his mouth and ears. Afterward he dried up and hardened. Then he must have been turned into the dullard that Jōsuke is today.' Some people expressed such views with utterly serious expressions, while others spoke mockingly. But the question of Jōsuke's past was no closer to a solution.

"The mother of the village headman had lived eighty long years and she became quite sick. When she was near death, she called her doctor and said,

'Now I am fully prepared to die, although until now, I have not known when my time would come. I have lived up to now because of the medicines you have given me. You have taken good care of me for many years. Please continue to take care of my family after this. My son is already sixty years old, but he is weak-willed and dependent. I worry very much about him. Please give him advice now and then and tell him not to let the family fortunes fail.'

"The son, who was the village headman, heard this and smiled bitterly,

'I am already old enough to have white hair on my head. By nature I am a bit dull witted, but I have listened to all you have taught and will do my best for the family. Please don't worry about this world of ours, just chant your Buddhist prayers and die in peace,' he said, but the sick woman looked at the doctor in some distress, and said,

'Just listen to him, doctor. You see the fool that has been such an affliction to me. At this point in my life, I have no intention of being reborn in paradise if praying to the Buddha is the only way to do it. If, due to lack of faith, I am reborn an animal and have to suffer, I don't think that's particularly terrible. Having lived so long and observed all sorts of creatures in this world, it seems to me that even cows and horses, so often made the symbols for pain, don't actually lead a life only of suffering. In fact, they seem to enjoy happy and contented moments too. Buddhism tells us that human beings are expected to live in a world far superior to that inhabited by cows and horses, but now that I think of it, I can count on my fingers the number of pleasurable moments I've had. And how I've had less free time each day than any cow or horse! Year in, year out, we have to dye our clothes new colors and wash them. Aside from such everyday tasks, at the end of the year, if we neglect to pay tribute to our master, it means punishment, for us a calamity of the first order . . . And just when we are beset by anxiety, along come our tenant farmers, from whom we expect payments in rice, to grumble about their poverty. Ah, to think people believe in paradise! Where? When? My one deathbed wish is that you not bury my coffin. Take it to the mountain and cremate it with no fuss. Doctor, please bear witness to my request. My last wish is that I not become like that Jōsuke of the Trance. Ah, everything is so tiresome. I don't want to say any more,' she said, closing her eyes and dying a moment later.

"In accordance with her last wishes, her body was brought to the mountain and cremated. Jōsuke of the Trance joined the tenant farmers and the day workers, carried the coffin up the mountain, and until the coffin had been set on fire and the corpse had gone up in flames, and until the survivors had collected the tiny bones which remained among the ashes, he busied himself as a substitute cremator. But when people realized that his zeal was motivated only by his desire to get as much as possible for himself of the special dish of glutinous rice and black soybeans distributed to the mourners at ceremonies for the departed souls, they thought him mean spirited.

" 'Forget about offering prayers to the Buddha to be reborn in the Land of the Lotus. Take a good look at what's happened to Jōsuke,' the villagers said, spitting at the mention of Jōsuke and admonishing their children not to follow his example. But some people said, 'That may be, but didn't Jōsuke come back to life and didn't he take a wife? This might very well be due to the beneficence of the Buddha, who wanted to fulfill a promise to him of a bond extending over two lifetimes between husband and wife.'

"Jōsuke's new wife—the former widow—sometimes got involved in knockdown domestic rows, after which she would always go running to her neighbors.

" 'What have I done to deserve such a worthless fellow for a husband? Now I long for those days when I was a widow living on leftovers. Why doesn't my former husband come back to life again like this one has? If he were here, we wouldn't lack for rice or barley and we wouldn't be suffering without clothes on our backs as we are now,' she said, weeping openly in fits of regret.

"Many are the strange occurrences in this world."

When I finished taking notes, the brief winter sun had already gone down. The professor had overexerted himself; he looked tired. The book was open and spread out on his chest. He had shut his eyes under the faint yellowish lamplight. He did not offer criticisms or expound on his perceptions, which normally would have completed the session after such a story. When I thought about the hour or so it would take for me to get home, I felt impatient and, hastily saying good-bye, I left the professor's house.

Professor Nunokawa's house was in the outskirts of Nerima and in the fall many of the trees in this area scattered scarlet leaves on the ground. For someone like me who was from downtown Tokyo, the site evoked visions, tinged with nostalgia, of the Musashi plains. The bus route, however, was far off and to get to the station I had to walk quite a while through narrow paths made within fields which were occasionally surrounded by bamboo groves and forests. In summer and winter, this route was an arduous one. If I went the opposite way, I would come out on a highway and, even though the next station was a long distance away, I would be able to walk along a brightly lit row of houses.

But as I was accustomed to this other route, I had made it my routine to take the narrow paths in the fields even though it was dark. In the two or three days that had passed since I had last come, the daylight hours had grown shorter and I felt I should hurry. Burying my chin in the collar of my overcoat and holding my umbrella low, I walked along the dark path as a light rain started to fall.

Because I had not traded views with Professor Nunokawa about that strange man in "A Bond for Two Lifetimes," Jōsuke's lifelike figure came floating vividly into my consciousness as if he were there right before my eyes. In the story, there was no mention of Jōsuke as he had been before he had gone into a trance, only that in his next life he had changed into a stupid country bumpkin and had married into the family of a woman whose husband had died. It was not clear whether "A Bond for Two Lifetimes" derived from some specific source or was an imaginative creation of Akinari's later years.

But as Professor Nunokawa had stated, if the young Akinari of his thirties, the author of the gothic stories in *Tales of Moonlight and Rain*, had written this, he would have doubtless woven a tale of quite startling eroticism about a pious priest who was unable to get off the wheel of rebirth because, before going into his trance, he had looked at a beautiful woman and, his heart greatly moved, been doomed by that blind attachment to remain forever ringing the bell in his hand. In comparison to what the young Akinari might have produced, the Jōsuke of this "A Bond for Two Lifetimes" was so unkempt and stupid that, with only a slight shift, the whole incident could be transformed into vaudevillian comedy.

But the Akinari who had written this story must have already lost the sight in his left eye and his old wife, Sister Koren,

probably had by then passed away. He must have been in an op-
pressed and isolated mood when he had composed this "Bond
for Two Lifetimes." His tone half ridiculed and half feared those
still smoldering, seemingly inextinguishable inner fires of sexual
desire which were as strong as his creative impulses.

At the end of the story, he might have been trying to hint at
the bizarre persistence of an old man's sexuality, which still
squirmed about like maggots. Akinari's story told of a man who
had once, perhaps, been a sage of high virtue and attained an
enlightened understanding of the most crucial life-and-death
matters. This man then had the unfulfilled sexual attachment of
a former life finally satisfied through another woman's body, by
returning to this world. This time, however, he had changed
into an utter fool who could not comprehend a single letter.

The author displayed his skepticism twice in the story,
when those old women, longing for their afterlife, mock the
Buddhist laws of cause and effect. He seems to despise the very
nature of sex, which goes endlessly around and around in a vi-
cious cycle, never sublimated by old age or by devotion to reli-
gion.

This reminded me of Professor Nunokawa, who had taken
in Mineko, so much younger than he. Stories were told about
how she had already transferred ownership of the old house to
her name, presuming that the professor had not long to live. It
was hard not to see similarities with Jōsuke's relationship with
the widow.

While I was thinking over these matters, I suddenly had an
unexpected remembrance of the last time I had embraced my
husband, the night before he died in the bombing. I thought of
how I had writhed in his strong arms, panting like a playful
puppy, and had finally withered with the pleasures of a desire so
strong that my body and soul seemed to have vanished. More
than mere memory, those sensations suddenly all returned to my
flesh. My very womb cried out in longing. A moment later, my
foot slipped, I tottered two or three steps and seemed dangerously close to falling down on my knees.

"Careful," a man's voice said, taking hold of my arm,

which was still clutching my umbrella. With his help, I managed to regain my feet.

"Thank you very much," I said, out of breath.

"Sometimes the bamboo roots stick out onto the road around here," the man said in a low voice and then asked, "Have you dropped anything?" and bent down to help me look.

He was right about where we were—on a path cut through a bamboo grove just halfway between the professor's house and the station; I could see the light from a house flickering through the thick stand of bamboo. I could not make out the man's face in the dark, and since he did not have an umbrella and his overcoat was wet, I asked him,

"Won't you come under?" and held out my umbrella. Without reserve, he brought his body right up against mine.

"Icy isn't it? And the rain makes it worse," he said, and with a chill ungloved hand, he gripped my hand to help me hold the umbrella.

Although I could not see his face clearly, from his voice and appearance he seemed rather old and shabby, yet the hand he put on top of my gloved one was soft like a woman's. I preferred men with strong, bony grips, just like my dead husband's and so I did not care for the softness of this man's. Strangely, I did not think of shaking him off and even felt the guilty pleasure of the cold softness of his palm slowly tightening around my glove. The man joined his outer hand to mine in carrying the umbrella and used the other hand to hold me around the shoulder. My body was completely encircled within his arms. We had to walk along entangled in this way.

In the darkness, I staggered frequently and each time he adjusted his hold on me, like a puppeteer manipulating a puppet. And, touching me on my breasts, my sides, and other parts of my body, he would laugh, but whether out of joy or sadness, I could not tell. I suddenly had the idea that he might be crazy, but that did not diminish the strange pleasure I took in his embrace.

"Do you know what I was thinking about when I slipped a minute ago?" I asked in a flirtatious voice that might have passed for drunkenness. He shook his head and embraced me so tightly that it became difficult to walk.

"I was thinking about my dead husband. He was killed by a bomb in an army air raid shelter in Kure. I was in a government housing area not very far away with our child and survived. You know, I wonder if my husband thought about me before he died. Now for some reason I long to know how he felt before he died. My husband loved me, but being a soldier, he made a distinction in his mind between loving and dying alone. I genuinely admire my husband's magnificent attitude toward life, but, up until the moment he died, did he really not see any contradiction between loving a woman and dying . . ."

The man did not answer my question, and as if to stop my words, he brought his cold lips against my mouth. Then, sadly rubbing my arms, he gave me a long kiss. As his cold tongue became intertwined with mine, his sharp teeth suddenly came against my tongue. They were unmistakably my husband's.

"Oh my dear, oh my dear, it's really you . . ." I called as the man pushed me down in the grove where the bamboo roots pressed hard against me, and then fell on top of me, all the while seeking my acquiescence. But his hands were indeed soft and cold, quite different from my husband's. Those hands groped over my prostrate form and, as I resisted, tried to undo the buttons of my overcoat. I called out weakly,

"I was wrong. You're not the one. You're not my husband."

He remained silent and, seizing one of my flailing hands, forced my fingers into his mouth. Behind his cold lips, his teeth were pointed, sharp awls, just like my husband's, which had passed painfully over my tongue so many times in the past. But the hands were different. My husband's hands had not been as fleshy and soft as a woman's. And his body also . . .

At that moment, I suddenly remembered the steamy, mildewed, invalid's smell I had confronted upon entering Professor Nunokawa's room. Was this Professor Nunokawa? The moment that idea crossed my mind, my voice called out totally different words, while my body sprang up convulsively like some stray dog.

"Jōsuke, Jōsuke! This is . . ."

Muttering these words, I ran full speed into the darkness.

When I emerged onto the brightly lit street in front of the station, my heart was still pounding from the vivid hallucination which had seized me on the dark path. A train had just arrived and a crowd of men in black overcoats on their way home from work came pushing their way out of the narrow ticket wicket, each looking as if he had been cast from the same mold. As I stood at the side of the wicket to let the group of men through, it occurred to me observing them, that each of them looked like an unimpeachably upstanding man. For me, a woman, they caused simultaneously a feeling of envy and a seering twinge . . .

I had ascertained that Jōsuke of the Trance was alive and well in these men. More than that embarrassing hallucination of what had gone on before on the dark path, this realization started my blood churning. It was an unsettling agitation that warmed my heart.

A Mother's Love

by Okamoto Kanoko

OKAMOTO KANOKO (1889–1939) writes with a passion that seems to teeter uncomfortably close to madness. Reading her stories makes one almost fearful of the crazed dazzle of feeling that must have tormented her during her lifetime. The oldest daughter of a large and well-established family, she married Okamoto Ippei, later a leading cartoonist. He eventually provided the financial and emotional security that enabled his wife to pursue her career. Their son Tarō is a noted Japanese artist.

Okamoto began her literary career as a poet. During a period of personal crisis, she turned for solace to the study of Buddhism and published a number of research works. The poetic and Buddhist influences are apparent in her writings, as is a penchant for intense self-analysis. It was only four years before her death that Okamoto published her first work of fiction. Just as her reputation was becoming established, she died of a cerebral hemorrhage.

The novella "A Mother's Love" (*Boshi jojō*, 1937) perhaps best shows off Okamoto's singular talents. About half of the work is translated here. It was written after her son had decided to remain in Paris to study art, while she returned with her husband to Tokyo.

Although many sociological studies have proven that the bond between mother and child is closer in Japan than in the West, surely the mother in this story, so desperately lonely for her son, experiences an attachment too desperate and extreme to be considered typical, even by Japanese standards. In this mother's painful aching for her boy, she goes over and over the condition of her psyche, checking inside her own head every now and then, and reporting the slightest change in mood she discovers there.

Although the mother remains fixed within a melancholy emotional range, Okamoto Kanoko is remarkably good at dissecting the minute details of her pensive, sometimes hysterical mental state. Her use of words to depict the finest facets of a delicate sensibility illustrates a particular strength of Japanese literature. There is not much plot here —the mother longs for her son on the first page and remains in a state of longing to the end—but the fragility and precision in every description seem awesome achievements.

Okamoto shares with other Japanese writers a keen awareness of the natural world. Precisely which flowers bloom on a given day greatly affects the mother in the story, and when the wind suddenly grows stronger (in the extraordinary passage about a walk on the Ginza), the increased pressure of the breeze at the mother's cheek causes her entire mood to change abruptly. A Westerner reading these descriptive passages might notice the short shrift given to ideas, but for a Japanese writer like Okamoto, the relationship of humanity to nature is idea enough, and that singular sensation of the strong breeze brushing against the mother's cheek is as close to Truth as she cares to venture.

She walked out into the garden in front of the entrance to her home and waited for her husband, Issaku, to join her. The strong gusts of spring wind had been subsiding since dinnertime, but were now completely quiet. The only traces of disorder were scraps and leaves that had been tossed about here and there. The trees and grasses in the small front garden stood up in an oddly formal arrangement fit for a display case. The shapes were carved out with special clarity by the bright rays of the sun just before dusk.

"Nothing seems to be moving this evening."

A sense of nature's magic went through her in that moment and she felt a flutter of nostalgia as she remembered how the evening skies of the European summer had remained bright even past nine o'clock. It was taking Issaku forever to come out. He would always decide to go back to the bathroom or start looking for something he'd forgotten after he put his hat and coat on and was all ready to leave. When they had been abroad, he had been just the same. She smiled to herself and thought, "Here he goes again." She made tentative movements with the heel of her shoe, tapped it on the hard pavement and stepped forward resolutely, testing out the five or six stones that led toward the front gate.

The gate was latched shut and ivy had woven a network of branches across the whole surface, even the bolt. The gate didn't get much light and so it was only now, when she came up close and looked, that she saw many new red buds on the ivy vines, creeping out with the stealth of a reptile's foot or blazing forth suddenly like sparks. For some reason, those new growths unnerved her and she let out a small cry of shock. She told herself that she shouldn't look back again if it upset her so, but finally her eyes were, against her better judgment, drawn back. The buds clustered together, strange, raw, compelling. And what was most female within her was deeply moved by the small hardy life that the buds possessed.

"It's hard to believe that even this vine, dry as a dead strand of hair now, will blossom when spring comes."

There was nothing extraordinary about this observation,

but the thought calmed her somewhat and she summoned the courage to stick out her finger and touch a small bud. Just this slight movement was enough to bring back memories of her son. Then the rush of emotion was almost too much and she leaned her elbow against the porch of the Western-style building near the side gate as she gave herself over to the sadness and pleasure that reflections about her son always stirred in her.

It was five years now that her son, who wanted to be a Western-style artist, had been in Paris. Five years back when she and Issaku had gone abroad, they had taken him along and when they had returned to Tokyo, the boy had stayed behind. Acquaintances had been endlessly impressed by these extraordinary arrangements; just this noon she had had a visit from a clever society matron who, during the course of her visit, made casual inquiries about her son.

"So young, and still you could let him stay in Paris. It's really admirable, the disciplined way you have brought him up. The exchange rate is pretty low, I've heard. Even some boys from rich homes have had to come home. It must be very hard on you. But of course, he'll be a great success in the future. You must be looking forward to that."

She remained silent while this middle-aged matron continued complimenting her about what an extraordinary mother she was and how good it was of her to make sacrifices just for her son's career. Actually she did have to cut corners quite a bit in order to pay her son's tuition. And being the oldest daughter of a rather warm, affectionate family, she was partial to praise. So she had just sat there during their conversation and let herself bask in the rush of compliments. Only after the woman left did her feelings change to something more like disgust.

She was really infuriated that the woman hadn't the sense to realize that she was not the run-of-the-mill "good mother." The whole incident became a most unpleasant memory. It was as if someone had taken the single sad, wrenching love of her life, the one she had risked everything for, and degraded it into something like a farcical, tawdry sexual encounter or a gold digger's story.

True, like any other woman, she wanted her son to succeed.

Only if he really made a name for himself would the world defer to him and let him live in peace. For that reason she wanted him to get ahead. But not for herself—no, not at all did she want him to work just so that she could be proud or satisfied that she had such a son. She was well aware that she and Issaku had lucky breaks to thank for a secure position within their respectable, accomplished social class. But her own experience among such people had not been so grand that she would advise her son to sacrifice or scheme his life away just so he also might have a place in that world. It seemed crucial that she get straight in her own mind just why she had let her son study in Paris. These were precisely the reasons she had not dared mention to the woman who had come today.

In the past, elaborate rationalizations for why she had left him in Paris had come to her with great facility, but now she wanted to sweep all meaningless abstractions from her mind. The struggle to find precise words for intimate feelings strained her, but after one last tug at the brim of her hat she blurted out, "What really happened was that we all, parents and child, were bewitched by that city."

Finally Issaku came out of the door and, painter that he was, narrowed his eyes and inspected the color of the sky.

"Have a look at that moon. What a fine evening," he said, and then as if to hurry her, he went out the side gate first.

She and Issaku went by bus. Before, she had always used taxis whenever she went out, but since her trip abroad she had started using buses every once in a while. The bus went pretty slowly, so she had the time to look at all the houses they passed. Just by sitting there and studying all the passengers around her, she could observe the complete change that had come over Japanese boys and girls in the three or four years that she had been away. What she enjoyed most was to be sitting down among these people whose eyes were all, without exception, the same color as hers.

It had been full of tension, that isolated life she had led among foreigners. Only someone who had been away and come home could know how wonderful it was to look left and right

and find only Japanese faces on all sides. And more than anything else, for a mother separated from her only son, the bus
gave her a sense of community where she could find some relief
from immense, lonely aching. The train was far too open and
spacious to help at all.

As the bus made frequent stops, there were complaints and
laughter accompanying its bumpy progress. More and more
street lights were visible when they crossed the hills that took
them from the quiet residential section out into the busy com-
mercial center. Then they came to the highest hill, the one that
marked the outer boundary of the residential district, and when
the bus turned suddenly downward, she looked across at a
whole sea of lights stretching from the center of Tokyo to the
merchants' part of town. The specks of light undulating like
waves and the flickerings of neon poured freshness and exuber-
ance upon her, as if she had just now been shaken awake. It was
an urbanite's excitement she felt, the impulse that made her
want to whip the bus like a horse to get to the source of the
lights as quickly as possible. But the bright moment of exhilara-
tion was not destined to last, for she remembered that her son
was far away, and her grim mood quickly returned.

When the bus approached the M school district, five or six
students got on and she saw from the insignia on their caps that
they attended her son's old school. Confusion, more than sen-
timentality, was the distressing feeling that assaulted her first
when these boys appeared. The long visors of their school caps
and the wide cut of their trousers brought back visions of her
son as a middle school student, recollections almost too much
for her already tearful, quivering eyes. She sank her chin down
into the collar of her coat, pretending that she was suddenly
cold. But when she swallowed softly, she tasted the salty bitterness of tears.

After finishing at his M district school and obtaining good
grades on his entrance exams, her son had entered Ueno Art
School. Shortly after, Issaku's work gave the whole family the
chance to go abroad. At first reluctant to interrupt her son in the
middle of his studies or to go against the advice of his teach-

ers, she had decided to have him stay in Japan until he graduated.

"I think they're right, don't you? You have to get the basics
down first before you can get anything out of studying in the
capital of the art world. That seems like the right way to go
about it. So we'll go over first and see how things are there for
you. In the meantime, you live quietly while we're away, and
work hard," she had said, feeling very sensible, and her son had
agreed.

However, when the time came and she had been frenziedly
making the preparations for her trip, there had been moments
when she would catch sight of her son, quietly going about his
usual routine, and the difference in their circumstances had
made her very unhappy.

"Life is so short," she had finally said to Issaku, "It seems
wrong for parents and children to be separated even for a short
while. We should do what makes us happy now and worry
about the future later. What do you think?"

"All right," Issaku had replied immediately. "Let's take him
along."

Their son had been trying not to show how much he
longed to go to Paris with them, so when he heard that they had
changed their plan, he blushed, trying to smother his excitement
with a small smile, and said, "Tell me what's happened. Tell me
everything."

And so, paying little attention to the future, they had gone
off together, the envy of everyone. After four years had passed,
they had all completely fallen into the tempo of life in Paris. Finally the time came when they had to go back home. It had
taken all her determination to leave her son there. Young as he
was, her son was passionately attached to the most avant garde
art, and thus greatly fond of the Parisian soil that had nurtured
it. He seemed to burn with a firm sense of himself as an individ-
ual chosen from the ranks of Asian artists. He had drunk deeply
of that artistic city's artistic society. To have taken him back to
Tokyo then would have been to remove a valiant warrior from
the field of battle or to tear two lovers apart (Paris had already

become her son's lover). The mere thought of such a thing had made her cold all over. These extravagant emotions she had displayed toward her son had proved to her that she too had it in her to taste the bewitching charms of Paris.

Even Issaku, who hardly took an interest in the trivial details of domestic life, had had an unusually serious expression on his face when he'd said, "An artist would give his whole life to study in Paris. I couldn't come here when I was young, so my son will stay here and do it for me."

Issaku's words had been utterly rational, but he had himself been as bewitched by Paris as she and her son. Paris—where life's most refined feelings of pathos, simplicity, or sincerity had come forth childlike, almost foolish, and without definition. Paris—where the bequests of an acute, austere, and wise culture had been scattered as if by a madman, leaving beneath a lonely sadness. Paris—where those impelled to devote heart and soul to truth's pain, beauty, and goodness could not help but be charmed and bewitched.

But this decision had not meant that ordinary rewards would be theirs at the end of the adventure. Whatever knowledge of art her son might gain through deep involvement in that city would not be something the woman of this afternoon and many others expected to be valuable for entry into ordinary prestigious, "successful" society. Neither parents nor son had had such expectations. Their emotions had been more piteous, like the terrible sadness of a cornered dog.

After all, she had had no choice. She and her son had to live apart.

When her son had gone to see them off at Gare du Nord in Paris, he had seen her tears and, through the train window, pressed into her hand the handkerchief he'd bought as a going-away gift with his small allowance. Thinking of him as he had been when, afraid, with a man's embarrassment, even to raise his head and show his tears, she sank into melancholy and also an anger so strong that in another age she might have risen up and challenged someone to duel with her.

But on whom would she take out her bitterness? To this she could at last find no answer. Her body merely went numb with grief.

"But I can't go bad," her son had told someone else when she had been absent. "I always have my mother's feeling for me in my heart. Ours is not an age that requires heroes. I could use my parents' money and enjoy myself. My mother cares for me so much that she'd never tell me to be a success. But I feel that her love will make me succeed."

For a while, the bus shuddered along the wide street with its numerous government offices. A thick darkness, like the dead of night, sent a reflection of her face onto the other side. At times, it was the face of a flashy young girl she saw, at other times, the face of a lonely mother. It was the face of a mother who, in the two or three years since her son had reached adulthood, had become accustomed to viewing the world through him. It was tiresome to stare at her own reflection in the far window and so she drew up her coat collar in a gesture against the cold and turned around.

She peered through the window's cold vapor, a covering much like the surface of a lake. There a large light blue government building shone out in the distant darkness. An imposing bronze statue was silhouetted against the building's light. The trees, lined up in front like bayonets of different sizes under inspection by the statue, also carved out fine silhouettes. These were the chestnut trees. She had been surprised to discover them in Tokyo during a walk she had taken soon after her return. She had been delighted to see those faint white flowers arrayed together like small candles. Paris was a marvelous city, making light songs out of grief and sadness, and cleansing the wounds of the heart. And the clear, deep blue European sky of early summer spread out like a love potion's spell. The profusions of white chestnut flowers everywhere had been small droplets from a world of dreams.

Once during the chestnut flower season she had shut her

eyes tight, then opened them suddenly and stared hard at the
flowers within the leaves. And without saying a word, she had
pointed them out to her son. Her son had also closed his eyes,
opened them quickly and gazed in at the flowers. And between
them there arose such a closeness that their bodies had shuddered.

In a thick, piercing voice, he had said, "Mother, we finally
made it to Paris."

An ice cream truck clattered over the macadamized road.

His words had a story behind them dating back to the time
when her husband, then handsome and fond of drink, had often
been away from home. His excessive, youthful ambition had all
but obliterated the timidity that had once been so much a part
of his character. He had pushed himself until an unfeeling hard-
ness marked his every move. And life had seemed to have charm
for him only in his own capacity for self-destruction. He had
come to believe nothing worth doing or talking about. She and
her son had had little money and sometimes not even enough to
eat. So she had tried to make her son stop his piteous crying by
speaking words of comfort, almost deliriously.

"Come, we'll both go to Paris someday. Let's take a buggy
ride down the Champs Élysées."

In those days, she would say Paris, not necessarily meaning
Paris, but Paradise itself. Not a religious paradise however. She
had just about come to the end of her rope with life in that cold,
cruel world where not a single soul would reach out a hand to
help a shy, sickly, immature mother who had no way to earn her
own living, and a starving little boy. They do not really understand, those who say that despair makes death the only choice.
To die of despair requires the enormous energy of stirring, moving, deciding. But real despair only piles on burdens of weak-
ness, leaving the victim helpless, stripped of thought, reflex, and
recourse.

The only thing she had been able to do in her exhausted
state was to prattle deliriously about some vague far-off hope.
When she had spoken of Paris then, she had only been delirious.
Delirium though it had been, the very fact that she had men-

tioned Paris meant she thought the city a good place. Or perhaps she had been influenced by Issaku, a young, poor artist,
who had so longed to go there. At that time, she'd had no plans
to go or not to go to Paris in the future. She hadn't even known
whether there would be any future for them.

But then, Issaku had completely changed his attitude toward life and applied himself to his work. And fortune had favored them in most unexpected ways. More than ten years later,
when the whole family had set foot upon Parisian soil, she had
seen their being in that city as perfectly natural. Still, she would
have moments when the whole miracle suddenly dawned upon
her and she would sometimes feel that the tides of fate were like
a dream.

But she had become used to the city. The sights and sounds,
the very touch of Paris would sometimes bring back afresh the
anxieties and bruises of those ten years, and then a healing balm
would sweep away the aches each time. Paris was that kind of
city. It made her look back on her past with both regret and nostalgia. How many times had she cried softly in that city and
soon after laughed out loud. But the time when the city had
most gripped her feelings was when she and her son had studied
the chestnut flowers, and the delirium of that terrible past had
come alive again.

"Come, we'll both go to Paris some day. Let's take a buggy
ride down the Champs Élysées."

And then her son's voice had taken over and he had said,
"Mother, we finally made it to Paris."

She had been certain then, that indeed they had gained
their revenge. She had gained revenge against something. The
chestnut trees had given assurance that revenge had surely been
theirs. And this had been reason enough to make her love the
city. It is a commonplace of storytelling to weave vivid tales of a
woman who seeks to avenge old wounds and then falls in love
with the man who has helped in her struggle. How well she understood that feeling.

But it had been necessary to go home, for she was very attached to the soil of her own land, and could not be away from

her native place for so long. All their traveling also had put a great burden on their finances and Issaku had been faced with going back to work. They had been able at least to leave behind their son as their keepsake, their tie to Paris.

Each year for as long as her son was there, the chestnut trees would blossom in their plentiful loveliness on the Paris streets. And so, even when he was alone, her son might utter those words in his heart:

"Mother, we've finally made it to Paris."

Now she felt like having a good look at the chestnut trees around the statue in front of the government building in Marunouchi. She started wiping off the mist from the glass with her coat sleeve, but then the bus suddenly shook them abruptly as it took a sharp corner and in that moment the bare chestnut trees and the statue swooped off into the darkness outside the window. She changed her position in her seat. Into the bus glittered the lights from the busy Marunouchi shops, blinding with the promises of night.

The downstairs of the Mon Ami Coffee Shop had just been redecorated and the light gave off an invigorating freshness. Even after the heating stoves were turned off, the glow generated by the customers kept the room nice and warm. From the pleasing blend of flowers, which were a bit ahead of the season, and the youths' fashionable clothes, also too flimsy for this time of year, it seemed as if spring had already arrived here. The people spoke to each other softly and the whole effect was of a genteel still-life painting. From time to time the lively sound of soda water bubbled through the collection of unmoving figures in the room.

Issaku, with his artist's sensibility, could go for days without noticing a person if he saw no reason to be concerned. But once he started to worry, he became a nuisance with the fervor of his attentions. Recently, he had noticed how depressed she was and couldn't bear to see her gloom. So he now was always taking her out. He treated her as if he felt she were ill, even trying to soothe and humor her until she would go with him.

But he was a simple person and went nowhere but the Ginza. And always the Mon Ami. He seemed to think that the academic atmosphere of the coffee shop would be enough to bring the return of her good spirits. He would sit her down, make sure that she had tea and snacks, and then go off into his own world, tasting the Western food or, in a mood of convivial cheer, making conversation with acquaintances at the various tables.

She heard him call out to someone and heard the same hearty greeting returned as an old man entered. This father was rearranging a cane at the side of his cape, and his thin young son, trying not to get poked with it, followed in after him. The old man's eyes, beneath his glasses, busily surveyed the scene, and immediately decided that with so many guests in the place there was nothing wrong with just going over and taking the empty seats at Issaku's table. There was not a moment of hesitation as he unceremoniously pulled over two chairs which were in the aisle and set them at Issaku's table.

The old man sat down first and had the boy sit down beside him. Thin and slouching, the son seemed to take great pride in the fine suit he was wearing, but, embarrassed by the patent leather sheen on his plastered-down hair, he pulled his neck in and looked down. It took his father's prodding to get the boy to mumble faint words of greeting. The old man spoke to them in a voice that had the assurance, volume, and refinement of one accustomed to lecturing. The loudness was not at all jarring. An academic well known for his social work, he let his voice convince everyone of his fully rounded character. He knew Issaku well socially, but professionally he seemed to be more interested in her, whom he was meeting for the first time. While he made small talk with Issaku, he searched for the chance to talk to her. Finally he stared at her, as if at an object of interest, and said, "I find it strange. You are so young. A modern woman like you. And a student of Mahayana Buddhism."

"Ah, not this again," she thought to herself, once more hearing the hackneyed comment that people seemed to feel obliged to make about her work. Maybe he deserved a decent reply since he was more educated and might understand her motives better than ordinary people. So she smiled formally and said, "Don't you think I stay young because I study Mahayana Buddhism? It's healthy and liberating."

An appreciative smile spread over the old man's face as if a student of his own had made a clever retort. He scratched his head.

"Ah, you have certainly got me there."

She fell silent, dismayed because her words had been taken as a joke. She could have kicked herself for answering so seriously. He of course immediately noticed her confusion.

"I see what you mean. What you've said is enough for me to understand what you want to say," he remarked humbly, to help her regain her composure.

And she felt sympathy toward him as well, almost apologizing with her bowed head for putting him in an awkward position. The old man, turning serious, seemed to look within his own being, and spoke almost to himself, "Yes, that must really be the essence of Mahayana Buddhism. Indeed. It is not easy for an ordinary person to see so deeply into it."

After discussing other matters for some time—her studies, his son, his son's schooling—the old man finally found his opening.

"Tell me about your son. He's in Paris, isn't he? He hasn't come back yet, has he?" he asked, thrusting his neck forward. Then he resorted to that kindly voice common to his type of social worker when wishing to get information about someone.

"How long has your son been in Paris? It's been quite a long time, hasn't it?"

Somehow she couldn't speak freely in front of the young boy about her son's study abroad, and Issaku again answered for her.

"He went with us to Paris in 1929, and he's been there ever since."

"So he was still quite young. Had he finished middle school?"

The old man seemed to place quite a bit of importance on middle school and was relieved when Issaku told him about their son's education.

"Oh, really? So he graduated from middle school and then entered art school and while he was there he went abroad, is that what you said? Well, if the boy was really interested in Western painting, then Paris was surely the only place to go."

"His teachers tried to stop us, saying he should get the basics down in Japan, but this one," Issaku pointed to her, "couldn't go abroad without him."

The old man then let a kindly glow flood his face and said, his voice full of praise, "Of course. Only son and all. That's completely understandable. But it was something for you to leave your son behind. And in Paris, which is so full of temptations. Quite a decisive step, to leave him there at such a young age."

After the spritely old man and his son left the Mon Ami, her spirits sank and she nervously reviewed every last word she had said to him. In their exchange about the perils involved in leaving a young son in Paris, she was less than proud of herself when she remembered her answer.

"If he's really the kind of boy who'd get into trouble from such temptations, he'd get into mischief even if we stayed there and watched his every move."

Didn't those words have an unpleasant flippancy to them? She hoped that the old man would forget that part, and then all of a sudden she remembered him saying, "It was really something to leave him there alone."

Her son was far away in a foreign country and she had returned to Tokyo. She became more and more vividly aware of the distance between them. She could not control the loneliness that spread deeper into her soul.

One night—it was another evening when she had come to the Ginza with Issaku and was sitting at a table in the Mon Ami —she rose from her chair after thirty or forty minutes and said, "Well, let's go. There's a lot going on outside."

Issaku only smiled silently as he took up the cosmetic bag she had carelessly left behind. He followed her out. The neon lights in the Ginza sparkled down flowers of brightness from their heights. On both sides, the glowing illuminations seemed to hedge the narrow valley that the streetcar trafficked. The neon lights worked their charms like intimidating, deceiving elves who had chased the crowds into that valley. There was a distinct muted hue to the young men and women who jostled by raggedly, tightly packed like storm clouds. The streams of people meandered along the pavement going in opposite directions, one stream flowing along the shops, the other along the street. Suddenly they seemed for all the world like an elegant, dazzling, snaking regiment of a joyous race of people on a postprandial promenade, reveling in their youth—a race of people seen nowhere else in Japan except in the Ginza.

The storefront lights of the shops selling fans, food, furs, silk braid, cosmetics, and picture frames glimmered on the pedestrians. At the occasional break in the line of people, gushing waters of light rushed down onto the pavement.

It was hardly a moment before she found herself woven into the crowd. Once she had joined its ranks, she seemed to calm down. "Why fight a crowd?" went a saying she recalled, "submit and join them." Crowds were as inexorable as fate to a resident of the city. The warm southeast wind pulled a faint mist to the city's gossamer sky and the stars above flickered with each new breeze.

It took just one strong gust of this wind at her cheek to change her mood entirely. She had been planning to go as far as Shimbashi and then take the first taxi home. Now that resolve seemed from some faraway realm in a stranger's dream. She turned and headed in the opposite direction, toward Kyobashi. Submitting entirely now to the decrees of the wind, she let her body move forward. She walked, slowly, against the direction of the crowd.

She was all instinct. Nothing more than the biddings of the wind, nothing more than her move to escape its moist touches impelled her to change her direction. Observing her behavior with curiosity, Issaku tried not to interfere. For he knew that while this yielding to impulse attested to her immense fragility, beneath there were sturdy, dependable instincts. As he had many times before, he now observed her with interest when she

abruptly changed course. Under a willow tree, he drew a cigarette from his pocket and, having lit it, followed her at a distance, smiling, like a swimming coach observing a child in the
water.

She was in a daze as she walked. In that bewildered state,
colliding with a pedestrian came as an annoying jolt. Or, when
another stepped out of the way in the same direction as she
moved, they both became flustered, not knowing how to avoid
each other, and so they just stood still in front of the lane of people going the opposite way.

Eventually she became part of one line of people moving
along the street close to the storefronts. At just that moment she
caught sight of the back of a student who seemed to have
switched into her lane and was about five or six people away.

"Ah, Ichirō!"

The words hovered dangerously on the very tip of her
tongue. But she stiffened, catching herself in time, her nerves
about to leap forth from her skin. She felt the fever within her as
her throat and cheeks burned.

How that boy resembled her son! Small, with a firm up-
right posture, he walked along quickly with his left shoulder
thrust up slightly, his head and delicate neck bent forward. And
even in the hair which grew down to his neck and hung out of
his student cap, he was Ichirō's double. If only she could place
her hand upon that serge cloth, she would in a moment feel
there the soothing warmth so characteristic of her son. She told
herself that none of this was true, but her nerves did not listen to
reason. And everything within her sparkled with a new reckless
life as her longing for her son vibrated to her very core.

"Papa . . . That boy. He looks just like Ichirō."

"Yes, there's something about him . . ."

"Do you mind if I follow him a bit?"

"All right."

"Will you come too?"

"All right."

Even when she hurriedly ran back to Issaku, she did not
take her eyes off the boy's back. Again, she dashed away from

her husband and followed after the boy at a swifter pace than Issaku.

Occasionally her son had come to the Mon Ami with his friends on his way home from art school and they had had lively debates there about painting. Sometimes just after he had left the coffee shop, she and her party would arrive there by coincidence and the waiter, whom they knew well, would inform them straight off, "Your son, your son. He just left. You can still catch him." The waiter would speak in a bright cheerful voice, as if he too had been infused with her son's spirit.

Then she would rush outside to see if her son was still in sight, even thought she had no urgent reason to call him back. Off in the distance, she might catch sight of him going quickly off toward home, after having said good-bye to his friends. Only then would she shout out to him. He had always been embarrassed to meet family members when he was out on the street with other people, and so he would not make an overt show of a warm greeting but would simply let his eyes convey his happiness.

He found it especially trying to meet his mother in a crowd, and she also felt similar embarrassment. So she would giggle like some simple-minded country girl and stare at her son closely, while he would bite down on his smile and look away, saying, "You're wearing your coat crooked again. It looks sloppy." This was his way of demonstrating their family intimacy.

Sometimes when her son walked with her, he would become irritated and say, "You're too slow. I'll go ahead of you," and he would walk on quickly.

Going ahead for some distance, he would wait there, and greet her when she finally caught up as if she were a stranger. He walked slightly pigeon-toed, and his student shoes would hit hard against the pavement as he left his straggling mother behind. The back pleats of his wide-bottom pants were additional teases, swaying back and forth, creases cutting into each other as they beckoned her along.

"What a coldhearted wretch! He's a fool. A conceited ingrate!"

She had boiled with such ill-tempered remarks but still had hurriedly chased along after her son. In this irritation, there had been a strange happiness as well.

Now another young boy paced in front of her. He did not walk particularly quickly, but had she not occasionally hurried, he would have gotten too far away. The speed she maintained this night was identical to the pace she had kept when chasing after her son. Within her was the same strange mixture of irritation and pleasure that had been her mood when she had pursued her own child. Mild tears welled up, and she knew that her eyes were deceiving her. But while chasing the boy, she exulted in a bright and lonely happiness.

The boy went speeding past without paying attention to either the fabric store show window with its new striped cloth or the row of show windows of the electric appliance store that displayed neoclassical designs. Her son would have paused to look at these enthusiastically. Instead, this boy observed the people on the dark road who gathered under the lighted restaurants. Each time he came to a street crossing, he did not wait with the rest of the crowd, but slowly and arrogantly walked straight into the auto headlights, inviting irritated honks from the drivers. She kept muttering to herself, "Why doesn't he stop doing that? What a barbarian." These words were followed in a moment by the deliberate whisper, "Ichirō!"

She could not quell her desire to transform this boy into someone else. Issaku looked to the left and right at the streetcar tracks. He put his hand on her back, protecting her only when they crossed. He started to lose patience and muttered words of annoyance to himself. She became as numb as a sleepwalker, chasing the boy, colliding into the masses of the East Ginza crowds, all the while whispering bewildered fragments. "He looks like him! That boy looks like Ichirō!" Issaku could not decide whether she was going too far or whether she was simply demonstrating extraordinary spirit. For it was just because of this romantic streak of hers that they had been able to go together on that bothersome world tour and had gradually tasted so much of life that there seemed little left for him to experience. Now he didn't care what happened to him.

But she was forever innocent, forever following straight in the wake of her emotions, and he felt somehow that she had taught him how to live. He rested one foot on a willow tree, slowly smoking his second cigarette. With his own eyes he had to see the next development, as if he were going to view a portion of a play after the curtain had gone down. So he continued to follow after her through the crowds, keeping a considerable distance.

Compared to the West Ginza, the pedestrian streets of the east side were more reminiscent of the old-fashioned mercantile district of Tokyo. The array of open stalls and the lights twisted on the green branches of the willows created the informality of a fair. Merchant-class men and women in neat traditional hair styles and wearing wide-sleeved overcoats milled back and forth.

The young boy wove his way through, stopping occasionally beside the open stalls. His forward progress was erratic. The new droop to his shoulder and his dragging feet bespoke boredom. By now he had had enough of this sightseeing on the Ginza streets, but still he seemed to search for more amusements. Both his hands were firmly dug into his trouser pockets; he brought them out to straighten his jacket. Then, swaggering, he went browsing along the avenue.

Worried that she might lose sight of the boy's erratic route, she followed him more closely, against her better judgment. At the open stalls where people were gathered, she determined not to lose sight of him. Gradually, the boy became aware of her presence, this woman with childlike face and dressed in Western clothes, hovering near him as he took in every stall along the way, even backtracking so as not to miss a display. He pretended to be looking back at the oncoming crowds, but this was a transparent cover for his repeated efforts to appraise her appearance and character.

At a distance Issaku was protective. He was the first to note that the boy was behaving oddly. Unaware of the boy's ruse, she continued as if she were not directly involved. By accident she met the boy's sparkling eyes straight on. Then, afraid of attracting his attention, she turned around in a panic.

With every inspection of the boy's face, another layer of her dream vanished. He was handsome, but he did not look like her son. In the muggy evening his cap went further and further back on his head, revealing more and more of his round, wide forehead. His high cheek bones, his slightly sunken cheeks, the narrow, round jutting jaw, all somewhat resembling her son's features, came together to form a face intelligent and mobile, with strong hints of Napoleon as he had appeared on St. Helena. His wide eyes, flickering with blue green hues, conveyed the limpid sensuality of a Murillo drawing of a young girl. And there was now a sense of red passion at his lips.

"What a mistake I've made!"

The fierce honesty of her longing for her son pierced through her. That intense desire, springing from the unknown territories of her consciousness, delighted at the mere sight of the coquettish boy ahead. Then she descended into self-loathing so burning and bitter that she might have been crawling her way through a pit of lime. She endured a blinding discomfort as she went along, but finally these conflicting emotions subsided, each in its place. Her grief, sorrowful and nostalgic like the churnings of a distant sea, floated her off again to a dream space, propelling her through the crowds.

There was a slight drizzle and at the corner, the sidewalk artists began to put away their stools. Perhaps this drizzle had begun a while back, since many open stalls were already closed and fewer people hurried along. A veil descended upon the lights and the neon flowed off in an obscure blur. The boy was now making sure that he did not get so far ahead that she could not keep up with him. When she reached another crossing at Owaricho, the lights reflected brightly off the wet tracks.

She dogged the boy's trail because her loneliness was so unbearable. But only the sight of his back stirred her nostalgia for her son. Otherwise his handsomeness served her no purpose. Crossing the tracks, soaked to the skin, she suddenly turned back toward Issaku, who was following after her in the drizzle in his usual unperturbed manner. His chiseled features, conveying firmness through the evening lights, were slightly wet from the rain. She felt guilty about her selfish behavior, and tapped her heel on the pavement to wait for her husband to catch up. But just when she thought she had lost sight of the boy in the distance, he emerged from the darkness of a corner building. And there he stood for a moment quietly, before he ventured an awkward inquiry.

"If you have some business with me, why don't we go and talk somewhere?"

Astounded, she stared at him. The face before her was still childishly young. In the boy's smile as he looked down at her there was both willfullness and embarrassment. Gasping, a mysterious fear penetrating her, she groped for words.

"Papa!" she called out, and went fleeing toward Issaku, who arrived just in time.

"You are Mrs. Okazaki, aren't you? I am the boy you followed in the Ginza the night before last. At first I thought it was strange that a woman was following me. I was even more puzzled when I realized that it was the famous Mrs. Okazaki, and finally it seemed that I had to say something before we parted and so I impulsively spoke to you. You must have thought I was a bad sort from my question and so you ran over to the man I immediately recognized as your husband, the painter Okazaki Issaku. For me, it was all quite strange.

"So after you ran away and I walked home alone, I wanted to meet you again more than anything. Even now I feel that I must meet you. I don't know whether it is because you are a famous woman writer or because I am partial to lovely older women. Still, there must be more behind why I want to see you. What I want to know is why you followed me that evening and why, at the end, you ran off, afraid that I was dangerous."

This is what he wrote in a letter which arrived two days after the incident in the Ginza. A letter from that handsome boy who looked like Napoleon. She could not decide how to reply to

the letter, and did nothing for two or three days. Greatly conflicting feelings tore at her. She hated herself for her longing for
the boy, for the stupidity of her emotion, for the bother, the
whole shame of it.

After that, five or six more letters came. The handwriting
clearly showed that the boy came from a good family, for his
Japanese characters were well practiced. His strong ego was
clear in the handwriting. Aside from the matter of his family
background, she caught hints of a fresh intelligence there. He
would put extra flourishes on the characters and just as easily
leave some out, showing a carelessness about the script that was
a common tendency among modern youngsters. The childish
places in his writing touched her heart. He wrote that his name
was Kasuga Kikuo.

Perhaps because she did not reply, his letters started to take
on more urgency. Using their encounter in the Ginza as his excuse, he became quite recklessly bold in his insistence that they
meet again. As a writer, her name appeared in print all the time
and she often received letters requesting interviews. If she started seeing all the people who wrote, there would be no end to it,
she said to herself, deviously refusing to confess her true inclinations. But the succession of letters from the boy began to work
on her heart. Over and over, she trembled with the shame of her
wild emotional behavior that evening.

Unlike others who had sent letters requesting a meeting, at
least this boy actually wrote as a natural result of her own actions. She really had a responsibility to reply. She was almost
under obligation to the boy, wasn't she?

But all this fancy talk about being under obligation to him
and the other excuses she made to cover her embarrassment
were sharply undermined by a spiteful voice inside her. That
persistent voice nagged on and on, saying that if she didn't want
to answer the letters, then don't answer them, and if she didn't
want to meet him, don't meet him. She vacillated back and
forth for several days, putting off her reply.

Then one day, the boy wrote her again with a more piteous
plea that wrenched from her all the fretful feelings she had to-

ward him. Seeing that she was so easily moved by the boy, she
resented the awkwardness of her position.

"He's making a fool of me. Why don't I answer just once
and give him a piece of my mind?"

Then Issaku, knowing well that if she began to get involved, there would be no end to it, promptly suggested, "I wonder if that's a good idea. You have such trouble with all the love
you feel for your own son. But then again, that night you did
start all of this and so maybe it wouldn't be a bad idea to
meet him."

Finally she didn't know quite what to do. Since she could
not forget the problem, her anger took a most mysterious turn:
she became very embittered against her son, whom she so painfully adored and who had caused her to fall under the power of
these complications in the first place. She was irritated at her
son, who knew nothing of what was going on, and was probably
quietly washing his face on a Paris morning. What vexing turmoil, what bitterness, this dear son of hers aroused!

About two weeks passed. Since the boy's letters stopped,
she thought that the matter had ended. Occasionally, she felt the
same regretful pull as toward one she had reluctantly parted
with forever. Perhaps she was actually extremely cruel at heart,
she thought to herself, and her shame at her own behavior intensified. Just then, another letter arrived.

"If you will not meet me alone, please meet me with my
mother. Both my mother and I would like some advice from
you. Please, I beg you to do me this favor."

There was a new appeal in this letter. She was delighted, as
if someone from whom she had unwillingly parted at some far-
off place had suddenly reappeared. This pleasure overcame all
the ambiguous emotions she had felt toward him up to now, so,
without much fuss, she immediately set about making an ap-
pointment to meet him. Issaku also had a look at the boy's letter.

"Why don't you try meeting him? His handwriting
isn't bad."

Suddenly she recalled the figure of the little Napoleon who,
that night on the Ginza, was both her son and another beautiful

young man, and his charm enveloped her like a cloud. It was a surprising discovery, this purely female, girlish side which emerged from the underside of her motherly feelings. While she was writing a letter to the boy arranging to meet him, the persistence of these feelings nagged at her soul.

She met Kasuga Kikuo in her elegant drawing room decorated with a simple arrangement of freesias. On the night of the day after he received her letter, Kikuo came from his house in Musashino to pay her a visit. The large gas stove in the room, its fire unlit during this season, was covered with a small silvery embroidered cloth. The velvet sofa, which she had brought back from London, had golden tassels on each arm. Kikuo sat in a dignified manner on the deep cushions of its seat. That night Kikuo wore a good Japanese robe with a traditional design. The pattern was quite sober for a boy of twenty-two like Kikuo. He looked dashing, elegant, and artless, as if he were a handsome Western boy wearing Japanese clothes.

She wore her uncurled, bobbed hair in a plain style, and a silvery crepe Japanese-style jacket. She marvelled at how quiet and simple her mood was. There was not a trace of the troublesome conflicts which had so disturbed her up until the time of their meeting. A boy with a razor-sharp will and an intellectual woman who could be quite charming with her show of mature matronly emotions (sometimes during the course of their conversation, the woman was a mother and the boy momentarily became the woman's son) passed a warm spring evening pleasurable to both of them. After they had met in this manner three or four times, she told Kikuo the real reason why she had followed him in the Ginza and he told her about himself.

Kikuo's father, Kasuga Echigo, had been too frank and too fond of argument for a diplomat. Naturally not much appreciated by his superiors and colleagues, he had been posted only in countries which had no international importance. Since he had not been at all busy with his work, Echigo had more and more been given to drink, long one of his amusements, and he had also pursued his own studies. Although he had lived in small countries, of about as much importance in the field of in-

ternational relations as the North Pole, he had taken an interest
in the state of the world and always had a vast supply of opinions.

His discontent with his work frequently intensified the stri-
dency of his utterances. He had moved from country to country,
and at about the time when he acquired the nickname The Eter-
nal Minister, he was forced to retire from the government, receiving the empty title Honorable Ambassador. He appeared
resigned to his fate and did not seem at all interested in com-
plaining about how he had been ill-used. He had decided to begin at last living the idealized life which he had been formulat-
ing in his mind for some time.

"I must taste real life."

A strained smile crossed Kikuo's face when he told her that
this had been his father's favorite sentence up until the day he
died. His father had chosen Musashino for his new home since
this place, of all the sites in Japan, had reminded him of his
birthplace. There he had built a luxurious Western-style house
and then he had married.

"He married very late. There was an age difference of more
than twenty years between my mother and father. My father
was over fifty. When I think about it now, he must have been
pretty egotistical to have brought a child like me into the world
when he couldn't have had much hope that he would live to
look after me when I was a teenager. My mother also swallowed
all her doubts and agreed to marry him," Kikuo said.

His mother, Kyōko, belonged to a wealthy local family. She
had been in many ways an ordinary woman, but she had just
been crushed by an unhappy love affair. She had fallen in love
with the son of the wealthy Oda family who lived in the same
suburb. Although himself rich, this ambitious boy had also been
interested in modern social issues and strongly inclined to take
up the ways of the common people. He had not actually disliked
Kyōko, but rejected her because she belonged to a rich family
and had been brought up in the coddled, overprotected fashion
common to that class. He broke with her just as the engagement

was about to be arranged and ardently threw himself into a marriage with a middle-class activist in the women's suffrage movement, as if he wished to prove some point about his principles and ideals.

After the drab, mousy little Kyōko had suffered a broken heart, she inexplicably turned into a brazen, shameless woman. Kyōko immediately agreed to marry Kikuo's father, who had become particularly fond of her classical beauty. Even though the father was almost an old man, Kikuo's mother was attracted to his background of long sojourns abroad and she also liked his gentle ways and the exotic traits in his character. The marriage had been concluded uneventfully in the luxurious Western-style home in the middle of a pine forest. There they had begun that domestic existence which for Echigo was "tasting real life."

"But is it really possible to go looking so consciously for the taste of real life?" Kikuo asked. "Is it possible to run around screaming that you're going to grab life and taste it? Didn't Maeterlinck say that the happiness of life is only a blue bird always flying out of reach?"

Kyōko, at first disliking her position as a figure set into the background of her husband's grand life plan, had felt pressured to fulfill her role. Even though her husband was old and permanently retired from the foreign office, she had expected that he would bring his own past experiences to bear upon their home life and thus give brightness and meaning to her existence as his wife. She had thought that this might compensate for the difference in their ages. But her husband had retained the manners of a cultured gentleman only regarding his coffee, which he ground and poured out by himself quite expertly every morning. Otherwise, he merely stayed indoors every day like any typical old villager. She had no choice but to resign herself to going along with him. In the prime of her life, Kyōko had gone out of her way to wear an old woman's hair style and clothing as she set about taking care of this old man. (Her rather warped, hysterical character seems to have been formed during this period.)

"Just before my father died, he would thrust his fishing pole

out from his study window and fish in the pond which had been
dug just outside. With a melancholy look on his face, he would
fish for carp and dace all day long. His arthritis made it difficult
for him to move and my mother had already begun to treat him
like a simple little child who might fly off into temper tantrums
any time. My mother rationed out one glass of wine to my father at each meal. When he coaxed her for one more, she would
refuse, saying that drink was not good for him. Then a big fight
would start."

When he came home from middle school, Kikuo would go
in to greet his old father, who would of course smile with happiness at seeing his son, to whom he would always say, "You must
do your best from now on to taste real life."

Enjoy life, he meant. Since these words had come from his
father's senile, wretched present, the boy had felt that the sylla-
bles echoed in the air as if brought forth from hell. When his father died, his mother felt that a great burden had been lifted
from her shoulders.

"An interesting thing happened," Kikuo said. His mother
began to socialize with both her lost love, Oda, and also with
her former rival, his wife, who had aged in quite an unremark-
able manner, producing two or three children along the way.
Kikuo's mother often visited the Odas for advice about Kikuo's upbringing, considering them among her few dependable
friends.

Kikuo himself had graduated from a municipal middle
school and entered the First Higher School. At the time of his
graduation, he had had some lung trouble and so delayed his entry into the university. He said it was due to his ill health that he
was now taking a long break in his education, but his lung problem had been completely cured long ago.

"My health is what everyone thinks is the reason," Kikuo
said, blushing in his ingenuous way, with a sly smile on his face.

"Have you started tasting real life, as your father instructed?" she laughed, but Kikuo gave a frank answer.

"I'm not so optimistic and selfish about 'real life' as my father was. But this is the time of my life when I have the strongest

potential to learn, develop emotionally, and work. I can't be
thinking just about going to school."

After that they met three or four times within a month. Although he had previously written that she should meet him with
his mother, during their walking tours of Musashino they had
sometimes passed quite close to his house, but he had not once
invited her in, nor introduced her to his mother. She thought
that Kikuo had some reason for this and she was in no special
rush for a quick meeting with his mother, but one day she asked
him casually, "You told me in one of your letters that you would
introduce me to your mother."

Kikuo looked troubled; his face colored. "You wouldn't
meet me on my own, so I was forced to do something under-
handed by resorting to a cheap trick like that."

"Is that what happened?"

"Please, don't embarrass me by bringing that old thing up
now. You've always answered questions in the women's magazines by writing again and again about your son, things like
how you educated him, haven't you? So I remembered that and
suddenly, since I was desperate, I had the idea that there was
nothing wrong with using my mother as an excuse."

"You wanted to meet me so badly?"

"You make me feel terrible, talking so much about this."

Since Kikuo turned redder and redder, she wanted to tease
him some more.

"But, for example, what if at that time I had told you to
please come see me with your mother. Definitely with your
mother. What if I had said that I wouldn't meet you without
your mother, then what would you have done?"

"In that case, my mother and I might have visited you together."

"And if your mother had asked me about how to educate
her child, I would have then taken over the supervision of your
education?"

Kikuo gave a long mischievous laugh.

"Why such a loud laugh?"

Kikuo became very serious. "It was not fated to happen that way. I believe that things turn out as they should, that what is appropriate, actually happens."

"Is it appropriate that you and I have become such good friends like this?"

"Yes, I think so. Because it is you, we have become close. If it had been anyone else, some other mother, not you, who had chased me on the Ginza, I might only have been annoyed, or have started a fight with her."

"Oh dear, what a naughty boy."

"You say that even though you chased me like a naughty woman?"

"Well, then it's appropriate that a naughty woman like me be discovered by a naughty boy. That's why we get along so well."

After taking a quick look at the yellow roses blooming in a hollow near the road, Kikuo hastily turned back to look at her seriously.

"Your husband, is he such an understanding person?"

"Yes, he's understanding."

"You respect him very much, don't you?"

"Yes, I respect him."

"Just looking at him, I get a good feeling about him. If I didn't like him, I probably" (and here Kikuo blushed) "would not have been able to come to like you in this way."

"My husband is another part of our very appropriate friendship."

"And your son also?"

"You ask for too much."

"Yes, I ask for too much. It makes me happy to have you say that I ask for too much. No matter what a fine face, lovely sensibility, or great intelligence you may have, if you had an unpleasant husband and a dumb child, then I would probably..."

As Kikuo seemed to have incorporated her beloved husband and son into his own mental world, she felt herself overcome by a strange love for this boy. Then suddenly she remembered her son.

"My love for my son is not just some primitive maternal feeling," she thought to herself, as her eyes filled with tears. "It's a love that inspires my sense of poetry, makes me feel the whole romance of life, has transformed the way I think about everything. Yes, the love for my son is greedy, asking for much. Maybe it's good, such a love, maybe it's bad, but there must be good in a feeling that seems to be so basic. It's hard to decide about whether a certain feeling of love is good or bad when it is different from everything else."

Noticing her mood, Kikuo asked, "Have I said too much?"

"Yes, you've said too much, and I'm glad of it," she laughed.

Kikuo also laughed out loud. Then the two of them suddenly became quite calm and quickly started to walk on. To upset what they now shared would have been quite easy but they both wished to preserve this moment of mutual sentiment. She felt refreshed and happy with this realization; in a low voice that twisted sweetly in her throat she sang softly as she walked, while Kikuo went quietly along beside her.

Kikuo's house had been built on the top of a slope rising out of the flatlands of Musashino. With its high roof, the two-story house gazed down on the Japanese-style buildings in the area. Ivy vines climbed intricately up the face of the red brick wall. From his experience abroad, Kikuo's father had been enthusiastic in his belief that English-style homes were the most peaceful. Even though he had recognized that perhaps the purely Japanese houses in the area would make his house stand out too much, he had finally ignored such objective considerations and resolutely set about building himself an utterly English country home. The profusion of English furniture, which he had used abroad, gave each room an aura of opulent power.

When first built, the house had risen in ostentatious contrast to the bluish hue of Musashino's fields, exuding a sense of isolation and loneliness. Gradually the ivy from Musashino's soil had enveloped the red brick walls, which darkened with the passing years. The colors from the grasses of the flatlands had blended with the house's exterior, transforming the structure into a huge, magnificent rock rooted in the earth.

Beyond the stone steps in front was a double wooden door. The vestibule was a bit dark. On one side was a stately, sober staircase that gave promise of a bright second floor. On the rust-colored carpet were cases of stuffed animals, apparently imported, and skillfully arranged at intervals were plaster casts of goddesses and a bronze statue of a warrior.

Kikuo's mother came out to meet her and then led her into the salon.

"You have been so kind to Kikuo," the mother said, half turning her body and lowering her head, a pose which made it easier to sneak a look at her.

But she could not point to this sly manuvering as a peculiarity unique to this mother, since any middle-aged woman might try to gain an advantage over another person. She responded with the usual greetings, and the conversation abruptly stopped there. It was a good chance for her to closely examine all the objects in the house. However, Kikuo's mother, anxious to observe the social proprieties, seemed very uneasy. Bringing in the tea and cakes, the mother tried to fill up the silence.

Her first impression was that the mother was a real beauty of the kind described in the poetic classics. With the so-called classical oval face and dark eyebrows rather close together, the fine features were fit for a painting.

"There are a lot of bushes around here, so the mosquitoes are already out at the end of spring. Do be careful," the mother said, making a gesture with her hand as if trying to sweep away something.

"This is just fine. I'll serve myself now, so don't trouble yourself," she said, gently putting her hands out to stop the mother, who opened a bottle of lemon juice and brought it toward her cup. "Why don't you just sit down here so that we can talk."

"Oh, excuse me."

The mother finally sat down on the edge of the sofa, tugged at her sleeves, and then arranged herself formally, pulling in her chin and sitting with her head bowed.

She began to feel irritated, and even started to suspect that the mother misunderstood their relationship and was demonstrating disapproval by such behavior. She thought she must do something.

"Kikuo certainly knows his own mind," she said and immediately afterwards felt that she had been too hasty in introducing the topic.

The mother appeared startled at the mention of her son and for the first time faced her straight on. "Do you think so? I brought him up alone after his father died and so I'm afraid that in so many ways I wasn't able to do all that should have been done," the mother said, and a sly look, pleading for both help and sympathy, appeared on her beautiful face; for the first time there was some display of vivacity.

At the beginning, she had doubted whether there was any resemblance between Kikuo and his mother. Now she saw where they looked alike—the mother had the same expression on her face that Kikuo wore when asking favors of women. As soon as this resemblance surfaced, she could see that the mother's good looks appeared in Kikuo's clean-cut features. The mother continued to look uncomfortable.

"He's intentionally delaying his entrance to college, and he's just wasting his time, doing nothing. And sometimes he says the strangest things. I cannot manage that child by myself. I'm very happy that he has made the acquaintance of a woman as accomplished as yourself. I wonder if you could scold him about this. I thought of asking your advice about his future education, but it is probably rude of me to ask stupid questions," the mother said, tugging her sleeves.

Her pity for the mother was mixed with an immediate sense of disappointment. Here was the mother of a son with such a complex soul as Kikuo's, and the woman understood nothing about him. A boring mother, this woman, servile and

wishing only a stereotyped tranquillity for him. Now she understood that there had been a good reason for Kikuo's hesitancy in
introducing her to his mother.

"I don't mind your asking me at all. There are many things
for women like us to talk about since we both have sons," she
said, watching the effect this would have on the mother. Her
anger gradually rose. At this point, if the mother were to continue in a timorous manner, she would have wanted to say
something like, "If you don't pull yourself together, I'll just steal
that fine son of yours away from you."

Completely misunderstanding her guest's thoughts, the
mother said, "I hope you don't mind my saying so, but I can't
really believe that you have a son. You look so young."

She felt a warm, sweet disgust at the word "young."

The maid came in, bringing melons to add to the food already on the table. Turning all her attention to the melons, the
mother said, "We got these from someone in the neighborhood
who loves to grow them," and "Take this slice, it doesn't have
many seeds."

She felt disappointed because the mother stuck to this triv-
ia, and she told herself to drop the matter. Her own son was important. She did not have time to luxuriate in worrying about a
stranger and his mother. But remembering Kikuo, whose soul
was like a green log smouldering, she could not but wish to help
the mother too.

While she listened to the murmuring of the leaves in the
trees outside the window, sadness dampened her mood. Out of
perversity, she fixed her eyes on a sparkling streak of light on a
portrait and then began to study the entire figure in the painting. The old gentleman portrayed had a thin, high forehead and
a large, sharp nose. He was dressed in a Western uniform, almost entirely golden braid. Although his French-style beard
went in a wide twirl close to both sides of his jaw, the man
looked exactly like Kikuo. She got up all of a sudden and stood
beneath the large portrait frame, bending forward slightly to
look up at it.

"Is this Kikuo's father?"

The mother came over to her side, as if influenced by her guest's actions. Almost automatically, the mother stood next to her and gazed at the portrait.

"Yes," the mother answered in a defenseless voice, and then added, this time with some spirit, "This isn't really a good likeness. He looks a bit old here."

Kikuo had told her all about the father's senility in his later years and so she thought that the mother was offering an excuse when she said this. It seemed that the woman was still unable to fully accept her own marriage to a man who had been so much her senior.

"He looks very dignified," she said sincerely.

"No, it doesn't look like him." The mother's voice was so full of a fierce hatred that she was surprised enough to look the woman full in the face. And what surprised her more acutely was that on the mother's face there appeared a desperate and vulgar expression which had not surfaced until now. Then the mother laughed out loud for no reason, a reaction which, when combined with the classical beauty of her face and voice, made a distorted and unpleasant impression.

The mother knew that her change in attitude had been noticed and seemed embarrassed at having been so carried away. She ran her finger through the side of her old-fashioned hairdo, and firmly scratching there, tried to regain her previous genteel and matronly placidity. But a muscle twitched wildly at the side of the mother's forehead, and the lines from her nostrils to the edge of her mouth deepened.

As a mere guest in this house, she wanted no part of the dangerous emotional situation looming before her, and so, as a distraction, she said, "Kikuo looks just like your husband."

"He may look like him, but the resemblance is only skin deep. He'll never become like my husband." Here the woman laughed ironically, and it was impossible to tell whether she was talking to her guest or to herself.

"You said before that you thought Kikuo was very strong minded. I'm grateful to you for this opinion. But actually, I think that Kikuo might be going bad. His reputation is not good.

He did well in middle school and in higher school, but after that he has been most unsettled. Maybe it's because his old father, up until the day he died, kept telling him foolish things all the time."

"Kikuo also told me about that, but I think now he is trying to make sense of it," she said, finally seizing her chance to get in a few words. "I think he's quite all right."

"Do you really? I think that even though he cannot become like my husband, I should help him get his life in order. I would maybe like him to work for a good, reliable company. Then get himself a wife from a good family and settle down. To do all that, at the very least, he must graduate from college."

She had felt uneasy before, when the woman had confronted the outrages her husband had forced upon herself and her son. Then the woman had seemed to be on the verge of a dangerous outburst, maybe on the point of uttering curses, but gradually calm prevailed. Pity filled her soul for both the mother and the child because the ordinary dreams which the mother had foisted upon Kikuo were so dramatically misdirected.

"Is Kikuo's engagement all settled?" she was suddenly compelled to ask, thinking this solicitous inquiry would interest both of them, since they were mothers of sons.

The woman colored with pride and answered, "Yes. She's the daughter of a family with whom I have some connection. The girl has a very endearing character. Of course, we parents hope that they'll end up together, but since the most important thing is for them to get along with each other, we're having them spend time getting acquainted."

The woman checked the reaction on her listener's face and added, "They seem to like each other." Then she left the room, preparing to serve still something more, and went to consult with the maid.

She gradually realized that perhaps the opportunism the mother displayed in fixing up her son with the daughter of her old boyfriend belonged to the same category as the woman's senseless urging of tea and cakes upon her guest. Just then, Kikuo came into the room with a mischievous child's expression of feigned innocence.

He had brought her there to the house and then left. "Somehow or other I don't think I can stand here and listen to you two talking the chitchat women always go through when they first meet each other," he had said with sly bashfulness and then made his escape to his study.

She had seen from this behavior that Kikuo had become accustomed to her and expected her affection. When she saw him now after having met his mother, she felt welling up from the depths of her heart great surges of emotion for this Kikuo, whom fate had brought close to her through her painful love for her son; Kikuo, who had come this far in taking hold of her heart; for this boy, who had become used to her and expected her affection, and whom she wanted to draw close to her and caress endlessly.

On another day Kikuo took her to his study, a large Western-style room way in the back of the second floor. A flower carving like those seen in the homes of the English nobility was embossed on the high ceiling. There was a huge mountain of books on the desk and above that a simple, old-style Greek clock hung on the wall.

There didn't seem to be any other decorations. The long lounge chair in one corner definitely caught the eye, although what country's style it represented was not immediately clear. Without hesitating, she walked over to lift up the cloth covering the books, but Kikuo waved her away, saying,

"I don't feel like discussing books today."

"But you read such a lot."

"That may be true . . ." Kikuo smiled broadly. "Because of that I sometimes really hate them. For days I just close them all up and the very sight of them makes me sick. Today is one of those days."

"That sometimes happens to you with people also, doesn't it?"

"I suppose that can happen. But since I have to live in this world with people, I can't come right out and show it."

"But you told me you had a girlfriend you liked and then you stopped caring about her. Yet you followed your mother's advice and got engaged to her anyway, didn't you?"

"Why talk about that? I didn't know anything about women then, so I was just curious."

"Does that mean that now you understand women and you're not curious about them any more?"

"When you talk like that I am sorry that I've told you about what happened. You seem different, but still you're a woman. Don't you see that a person changes after reading books or getting older or having experiences?"

"That's true, but a person's most essential values and tastes don't change, do they?"

"That's true. So if people don't agree on those essentials, they soon lose interest in each other."

"That makes sense."

"Do you think so? It's the same with books. There are books that make you feel troubled, but still you can't tear yourself away from them."

"Has that happened to you recently?"

"With Shestov. I really suffered thinking about Shestov's void. For a Westerner, the void comes out of the assumption that there's an act of negation. It's a concept that excites me tremendously because there is so much feeling in that act. But it's not a totally intellectual thing. For Asians, the void is very cold, colder even than nature. If both these voids have their faults, where is it 'that we should go'?"

"You're talking about Eastern ideas of the void found in Lao-tzu and Chuang-tzu," she interrupted. "That void is completely different from the 'emptiness' or 'nothingness' advocated by Mahayana Buddhism. In Mahayana, you accept everything and come to appreciate a stark nothingness. It's free-flowing and without obstacles—a thing that draws out the full range within you. Then all life begins to radiate—marvelously and with spirit. But young people enjoy nihilism. Affirming life seems old-fashioned, but nihilism somehow sounds fresh. Rather than using one's brains to make use of life's many resources, it's much more simple and comfortable simply to choose nihilism."

"You make me realize why I was drawn to Shestov, even though I hated reading him and he was so difficult to get all the way through."

The maid brought in tea and put the cups on a space between the books on Kikuo's desk. After the maid left, Kikuo gave a cup to her and, drinking himself, said, "Today my mother's not at home, so there's nothing good to eat. But we won't be bothered by her besieging us with food."

When he said this, she thought that the excessive offerings of food might be his mother's real charm. The hospitality had annoyed her because the mother had not expressed any real feelings in her behavior and so the formality of the occasion remained prominent, making everyone feel uncomfortable.

"Your mother . . ." she was adding.

"Well, let's forget about my mother," he put in. "You said you wear kimonos in the designs and colors that your son tells you to wear. The black and red combination on your neckband also?"

"Yes."

"Hmmmm. That's really a unique way of expressing a mother's love."

She turned out the light near her pillow. Out into the darkness of the night, she tossed away Kikuo's letter, which until then had been beside her cheek on the pillow. A ray of light from the lamp, which she had been steadily and sadly watching since finishing reading Kikuo's letter, now pressed in on her eyes, closed in the darkness. Within her eyes, the light mixed with the memory of Kikuo's handwriting. She could not get to sleep. Kikuo's letter held the echoes of what he had mused upon after the short period of suffering since they had stopped meeting each other.

"You said that even if it was unconscious, you could not tolerate watching your motherly feelings draw you close to a young boy like me, since our relationship developed as a direct result of your love for your son. People might criticize me and say that I became close to you in order to satisfy my latent, unsatisfied longing for a woman and I started to believe that myself.

"Since your fastidiousness does not permit you to sully your maternal feelings for your son, I also think that for me to bring any stain upon that fastidiousness would be inexcusable. I can understand now why I must make a clean break with you. But I would like you to let me say something now. When I look back on it, I can clearly understand why we cannot continue to meet without confronting the obvious male-female elements of our relationship. Please believe that what follows is not sourness. I feel, however, that it shows shallow thinking to immediately attribute what we feel about each other to Freudian sexual instincts. Why? Because actually the essence of our relationship is at a place deeper within us. What we feel for each other is located much closer to the very core, where it can't avoid melting into the absolute of the void.

"Yet, we are attracted to each other like plus and minus, in that for you the void is something you have gotten from your learning, while for me the void is some dry, hard shell which I carry on my back because of the great pulls of my ego and passions. I had faint hints of a potent force within you. It is difficult for me to explain further in a letter, but if I force myself to put this down in words, your emptiness is—that bright and shining emptiness—that emptiness which makes you certain of the consciousness of your existence—that void which is inspired by ecstasy—in nature, by a keen awareness of a flower's stem in the slightest breeze—in the human world, the mysteriously graceful and endless void which brims over when one is in a kind of self-induced trance . . ."

She felt the black red vine of Kikuo's passion which, while forcing itself into that shell which was his void, still struggled to make its way out to the light. The tip of this vine tried in vain to emerge and only succeeded in burrowing inward. She felt that it was selfish and sad of her to think only of purifying her own

soul, and to stand by and not hold out a helping hand to him
while he endured all this torment.

She remembered an oppressively sultry and lonely period
of agony during her own girlhood. (One of her childhood poems
read, "I came to the mountain twenty days ago, but there is not
one tree warm enough to console me.") Spiritually abandoned,
she had been left with her rich flesh that had cried out in frus-
tration. And she had sensed Kikuo's flesh with immense clarity
that day and had, without warning, left him at Musashino. That
was how, in the end, she had parted from him.

On that afternoon close to the beginning of summer, the
two of them had emerged from his study and again started to
take a leisurely walk in Musashino. Once, the sun went behind a
cloud and the surrounding scenery darkened. But for the rest of
the day, the whole sky brightened up. The new buds on the tree
raised their drooping clusters and dispersed faint, volatile aro-
mas. The path they had been on began to head downward, and
then they walked on red, moist earth that yielded pleasantly under their heels.

Kikuo had still been talking about Shestov. He had fallen
into that brusque manner he assumed to cover his embarrassment whenever he was really talking about what mattered most
to him. As was his habit, he arched his back in the way that
seemed so full of his own particular gloom. He kept gesturing
with his right hand.

"Even if it is not the void, nor the limitless absolute, if it has
no charm or grace then we humans will find no appeal in it."

Kikuo had begun talking apparently to himself and she had
been unable to understand his meaning. In the end, he smiled
bitterly, pulling in the narrow pointed chin which reminded her
of Napoleon's sad fate during his last years. There was a narrow
gold inlay in one of his teeth.

Suddenly she felt tremendous compassion for Kikuo. This
uncontrollable compassion unintentionally showed in one of
her actions. She plucked at a prickly tuft of nettle which had
stuck to Kikuo's chest. His high school uniform fit so tightly that

the buttons were about to burst. His pectoral muscles were so developed that the line of buttons had formed a vertical valley. Through the blue serge fabric she seemed to feel the vain grasp of his soul, which had urgently wanted to ask something, then had been at a loss at how to ask. A searing passion had risen within her like an all-embracing fog. She had wanted to envelop this boy with something gentle and yielding and waft him off into the clouds.

. . . Without saying a word, she . . . his hand . . . That was all there was to it, but . . .

She had turned away in a wild flight from Kikuo. Until she reached a highway in Musashino, she had run at full speed, turning at a gentle downward slope within a grove of trees and passing by a thick growth of plume poppies. Part of a field where pale white wild camomiles were in bloom had come into sight and at the end she caught the scent of mint leaves. On a highway near a group of houses, she flagged down a taxi and went to her home in downtown Tokyo.

Her face was so white that the maid looked at her curiously. As if sick, she went to her room and sat down at her desk.

"I won't see him again. I won't see him again," she said to herself and wrote Kikuo a brief letter breaking off their relationship.

She was genuinely surprised that a husband and wife could discuss such matters, but late that night she gave Issaku the rough outline of what had happened between her and Kikuo.

"Ha, ha, ha, is that so?" he laughed. "Ha, ha, ha, is that what happened? Because of him, your frenzy about Ichirō has been a bit relieved. I think you'll be seeing this Kikuo occasionally, and your anxiety about Ichirō will ease up. You'll feel calmer and do some work." He lit a cigarette and with a light smile on his face gazed at her. "You don't feel you've betrayed Kikuo's fiancée or me. What's interesting is that you only feel you've betrayed Ichirō."

"I definitely had a vague feeling deep down somewhere that I had betrayed you and Kikuo's fiancée. But that was only a

simple moral betrayal. So my feeling of betrayal there was not
so strong. But with Ichirō the betrayal touches upon the very
quivering skin of my most fundamental instinct. After all, this
problem started mainly because of my son, and so it's natural
that how I have betrayed him, my son, becomes most central
to me."

Having said this, her eyes filled with tears. There was no ex-
plaining it, but there was more than morality or obligation or a
yearning love for Kikuo. Her most profound maternal instincts
had not wished to defile her son. She realized then, so late, that
it had been that fastidious, sensitive, most instinctive of female
impulses, the attachment of a mother to her child, which simple
words like "betraying my son" did not really express. The relationship with Kikuo had developed because of her son's existence . . . and this had enraged her maternal instinct. The rage
of her motherly instinct, which would not permit even the
slightest stain, had insisted she flee in anger from Kikuo.

One day three or four years later, after she and Issaku had
returned from an engagement, their houseboy spoke to them in
a rather agitated voice.

"A Parisian painter friend of your son's has come. He
came straight here from Tokyo Station. He still had his bags
with him."

She immediately realized that this must have been K.S.,
an internationally known name among the present avant-garde
artists in Paris.

"Has he come alone. Or, has his wife . . ."

"A woman was with him."

If she wasn't mistaken, K.S. was on his honeymoon. The
houseboy brought out her son's letter of introduction which K.S.
had brought along with him. In the brief formal note their son
asked them to look after K.S., whom he had mentioned in a previous letter.

"And then were did they go?"

"I told the taxi driver to take them to a hotel. I told them all
about how you and your wife were not at home now."

Issaku, whose spirits had brightened, teased the young boy.

"When you say you told them all about it, what do you mean? You must have had a time of it. What did you do? Use your grade-school French?"

"No, both of them spoke in English. So I thought it was the first chance for me to practice my English in a long time. I really gave them quite a show," the young boy laughed and ran his tongue over his lips.

Since there was no more to tease the houseboy about, Issaku immediately started to think about how he could introduce K.S. to the Japanese art world.

"I wonder if he brought some pieces along so that we can have an exhibition?"

"Anyway, let's go and show them the Ginza or somewhere," she said, "and take them out for a Japanese meal. Why don't you call the hotel now."

"All right. You'd better bring his bride flowers or something."

She quickly changed her kimono. Among the big names in the Paris art world, K.S. had been particularly friendly with her son. She knew that he had not acted superior to Ichirō, but seemed more like a big brother. Naturally parents would like to do favors for someone who had been so good to their son. But she worried that if she, as a mother, left K.S. with a bad impression, K.S. would hereafter be influenced in his views on her son. Above all, she thought that she would have to take great pains with his wife, a woman like herself. Her son always thought about his mother and was strict with her when they were together. But behind her back, he was proud of her. Filled with warm nostalgia he may have praised her and probably spoken grandly to this artist and his wife about his mother. While she was dressing, she kept telling herself that she did not wish to betray the image of his mother which her son had given to K.S.

Although K.S. was younger than they had imagined, he was a highly intelligent gentleman. His attire was like a proper businessman, but in his nervous concern about other people's feelings and his extreme solicitude in turning down offers of kindness, he showed all the signs of a timid artist. His young wife stayed at his side and gently smiled, like a sweet flower in bloom.

At the Japanese restaurant in the Ginza where they soon took the couple from the hotel, the Westerners and Issaku thrust their legs into the sunken floor-pit under the dining table while she alone sat with her legs folded beneath her. Through the branches of the willows outside, they could see the evening crowds in the Ginza.

"The night before we left, Ichirō came to our place to say good-bye and we talked well into the night." Showing the good judgment that the best present to parents was news of their son, K.S. kept talking about Ichirō, saying over and over, "He's really doing fine."

The young wife, handling her chopsticks with dubious skill, laughed from his side. "That Ichirō."

A sharp pain stabbed her heart when she suddenly feared her son had done something to warrant this muted laughter. She wanted to find out from the woman's laugh whether she ought to protest. When she stared at the wife, the woman was already looking down, searching around in her soup bowl with her chopsticks.

"Has Ichirō done something?" Without thinking, her voice got louder, and quickly K.S. gave a short explanation to ease her anxiety.

"It was just after we got married. Ichirō came over and we argued about art while drinking beer until late into the night. I won't go into all the details but there is a new group of painters in Paris who call themselves Abstractionists. Within the group, there are sharp differences in what they emphasize. We were talking about that. Soon Ichirō was curled up in his chair and fast asleep. To show our respect for this Japanese artist, we gave him our bed. I mean, the two of us carried him in and put him to sleep in our bed. We drew the sofa and chair together and we slept there."

"Oh," she said.

"Wait, there's more. In the morning, he woke up. He looked puzzled when he realized that he was not in his usual place.

When he understood what had happened, he put on a serious face and said, 'Excuse me for getting in the way of the dreams of a new bride and groom,' and then he went home."

Then his wife laughed again, looked at her and sent over a smile full of kindness.

"Ah," she said, once again, and was about to smile. Imagining her son's performance, Issaku smiled as if to say, "I admire his presence of mind."

Her feelings seemed twisted up with a laugh. She had the kind of personality which was easily misunderstood, and while she could make strong allies, she also had the troublesome fate of making strong enemies. But her son was loved everywhere he went. He went about his life without inhibition and everywhere built himself a world where his spirit roamed freely.

The trials of youth serve a person later on. He was her son, but she could not help admiring him for not turning out to be a resentful boy but one who had changed his early trials to embellish his life. Her son must have been born with something pure and sturdy at his core, she thought. For some reason a feeling of gratitude welled up in her and in order to express it she looked toward no one in particular and said, "Thank you." She bowed her head in a clumsy Japanese gesture in front of these Westerners. Issaku too was drawn into her mood and bowed his head slightly.

The exhibition was full because Issaku's method of publicizing K.S. had produced results and, more importantly, because it was a rare chance for people to see originals of the latest Parisian art. On the olive-colored walls were hung seven or eight oil paintings and about thirty etchings. Many people were crowded together, trying to get a look. It was close to evening and stuffy in the room. The faint white light from the chandelier seemed a clouded, milky color, while the fronds on the potted palms shook slightly. There were several groups of painters standing talking to each other in the room, away from the crush of the other guests. Some French visitors had cornered Mr. and Mrs. K.S. and were addressing them intently. Issaku was walking around the room discussing with a critic the paintings to be used to illustrate a magazine article.

She made herself small in a chair, all by herself in the middle of the room. She looked at K.S.'s paintings flickering into view through the crowds of visitors. He presented material objects with a mechanistic regularity, but his style was powerful, romantic, and persistently human.

Since she had come into the room, she had been observing the movement of the crowds in front of one wall. Her heart had danced as she stole nervous glances in that direction, for there hung the one small sketch by her son which K.S. had brought with him. What made her nervous today was that the crowd was passing the work by, where usually people clumped together in front of it with a buzz of conversation. She looked at the line of people and felt extreme discomfort, as if she were watching a strangely smooth flow of water after wild floods had washed away a bridge's foundations. What had happened? Had they become tired of her son's sketch? Had it lost its charm for everyone? She couldn't stop feeling anxious, and without thinking she stood up to have a look. Through a space in the crowds, she could see only a blank wall. Her son's sketch was not there. She rushed closer. It was no optical illusion. There was no trace of her son's sketch. Only the title card turned over to face the wall.

"What happend to Ichirō's picture?" she kept saying, going around and around the room. Then she finally had an idea and went over to the sales desk at the entrance. Breathing with some difficulty, she posed her question and the young clerk in Western clothes looked surprised and apologetic.

"Wasn't that one for sale? Mr. K.S. thought that it would be good to have at least one painting stay in Japan and so he put a price on it."

She felt that pleasant warm water had been poured over her after being unhappily doused in a cold bath. Her astonishment soon turned to calm.

"Who bought it?"

"Someone who said he was leaving by tonight's train. He

said he wanted to carry it back himself, and because we were about to close, we wrapped it up and gave it to him. Just a minute ago. Here's his name." Written in the sales book the clerk brought out was the name Kasuga Kikuo, in the same handwriting she knew so well.

Without thinking, she ran out of the exhibition hall. She saw a throng of people moving from the elevators. These people were tired of waiting—all the descending elevators were full. As the crowd parted, she saw a young boy in an overcoat carrying a package wrapped in brown paper, going down the staircase. It was Kikuo. She was aware, as she looked at him going away, that he knew she had seen him. She felt rooted to the spot. She just stood there; all she did was think to herself, "Kikuo really does strange things." At once, an ache began to seep gradually into her flesh and bones.

She rested at her desk in her own room for the first time in a long while. She was rather tired from seeing Mr. and Mrs. K.S. safely off on their return boat to France. Then she opened a letter. It was from Kasuga Kikuo.

"I haven't written you for a long time. I now live in a residential neighborhood in Sendai City. I kept thinking about that 'nothingness' you talked about, which was to be found in a self-sufficient active life. I wanted to try and research proof for that theory. Probably I should have turned to philosophy, but considering how things are these days, I chose to get involved in a purely scientific field—theoretical physics. I entered the science department of Tōhoku University that fall after we stopped seeing each other. I am now a research assistant. During spring vacations I went to Tokyo and immediately came back here. The results of my research will be my graduation thesis. I'll do some more research and make it into a book. I'll send you a copy then, but I won't write about that now. Instead I must inform you of my mother's death three years ago. Other things have also happened. You remember the fiancée I told you about? We decided not to get married, at my request, so I am still single.

"I know that you were standing at the top of the stairs and

saw me among the people at the Ginza department store where
they were showing K.S.'s works. I thought I should explain to
you why I bought your son's painting. That's why I am writing
after so long. I won't write to you again. I want you to know
that my life is going along normally and you should not worry. I
bought the painting thinking, 'It's amazing that there is a child
in this world who is so miraculously fortunate. Such a son's
drawing is surely a rare prize and so I will hang it on my wall
and look at it.'

To Mrs. Okazaki. From Kasuga Kikuo."

She did not think that she should reply to this letter. What
was the point? But Kikuo. Kikuo. Although they no longer saw
each other, she had not put Kikuo out of her mind. Deep within,
just at the edge of that core where dwelled her exacting, chaste
maternal feelings, remained Kikuo's form, giving off its fra-
grance, spreading out, causing pain. Should she once again try
and insert Kikuo into that core? She had sent her son off into
adulthood. She had suffered because of her maternal feelings.
Now should she hold out her hand to Kikuo?

> When clouds cross your path, won't you ask the clouds
>   about me?
> And if you go where the snows fall, ask the snow as well.
> Since you have gone, darkness has filled my heart,
> Black is the night snow others call white.

Crabs

by Kōno Taeko

KŌNO TAEKO (1926–) writes of a situation that is very familiar to Westerners. Her heroines are middle class, inhabit a territory close to the borders of neurasthenia, and long for the end to a grim succession of unsatisfying days. They receive little consolation from their male companions whose attitudes often range between long-suffering and aloof.

Kōno is at her best when she speaks for the complicated and modern intellectual woman who wants independence, but suffers in the emptiness of a life without love. In the story "The Last Time" (*Saigo no toki*, 1966) her heroine considers what she would do if imminent death were upon her. She takes up such matters as final instructions to the milkman and proceeds to draw conclusions about her married life. Pressing herself to sum up, she decides that the bond with her husband has been mere sham. In her moment of understanding, she speaks for many of Kōno's restless heroines: "I want no part any more of living in the belief that my married life is a true marriage. At the time of my actual death, I would like after all to feel something at the end. And if this means I will leave the world with regret or lingering attachments, I don't mind. For only that will prove I lived a full life."

"Crabs" *(Kani)*, which won the coveted Akutagawa Prize in 1963, is another examination of a married woman's emotional discontents. The controlled prose compels regard, for an old theme gathers fresh power here with a strong Japanese dose of restraint.

T HE rest cure which Yūko had pressed for so vehemently had brought a marked improvement in her health. Even though only ten days had passed since she had come from Tokyo to the Soto-Bōshū coast, she could see the difference already. The old sluggishness and ineptness had disappeared completely. She was definitely aware of strength returning with every passing day. When spring arrived, she felt that she had begun to live again.

Kajii, Yūko's husband, had accompanied her to the resort. On the way, just as the sea, which they could only glimpse between clusters of houses and cliffs, burst into view, he emphasized his point again.

"Remember what you promised. It's only a month, no more."

From the first, he had simply not been able to understand why she insisted that she needed a change of scene. When she had brought up the idea the first time, he had taken it as a joke. Then, seeing that she was serious, he had just looked at her, dumbfounded. He asked her why she insisted on undertaking such an old-fashioned remedy when she was in the midst of a tuberculosis treatment with special drugs that were a hundred times more effective.

Then he gave her more definite reasons for opposing her plan. Even if she lived in an inn or boarded with a family, he would need to spend a lot of money, and while he wouldn't mind using all those funds if it meant that she was going to get better, to go to all that expense for minimal results seemed ridiculous. If it ended simply in a stable condition, that would be tolerable, but what if, by undertaking a treatment not prescribed for her, she should suffer a relapse just when she was coming along so nicely? At the very least, she would be sure to get depressed living in a lonely place away from home. He pointed out to her that no matter how good the air might be, if her mental state were shaky, there was no chance that her physical condition would improve. He spent a long time opposing her wish to waste all that money on such a foolish scheme.

While Yūko could see the rationality behind Kajii's arguments, she could not give up the plan to go away for a while.

"I think I'll be completely cured if I go. I'm sure of it. I know that you feel I'm just thinking of myself, and I'm sorry, but please let me try it for a little while," she argued with a blind tenacity.

At the end of autumn three years back, Yūko had begun spitting up the small quantities of blood which marked the start of her illness. That winter had passed without her being aware of it because, being hospitalized for the first time in her life, she was consumed by the sense of panic at the disaster which the sickness's onset had seemed to her, and by the expectation of the miracle cure. She had thought of little else. Last winter, Yūko sang the praises of the wonders of modern medicine and was constantly expressing her gratitude. The treatment was working as expected. There were no side effects from the injections. The swallowing of so much gritty para-amino acid into her system had been a matter of considerable concern to her, but it proved to be harmless and there was no sign of the drug hurting her intestines in any way. In fact, it was clearly evident every time she had an X ray taken that the foci of her disease, which were like three thick branches facing outward in the middle of the right lung, were gradually lessening.

"For a patient taking the medicine, you've done unusually well," the doctor said. "I'm very pleased."

Ever since fall—and she had been advised to wait until then—Yūko had been well enough to become an out-patient. Kajii had been having the old woman from Takaraya, a long-standing cooper's shop near their apartment complex, come in to do the cleaning and laundry twice a week, also to make dinner on those days and prepare the bath. After Yūko came out of the hospital, the woman continued to come in and do the heavy work while Yūko gradually resumed the household chores herself.

More than most people, she was prone to catch colds and she would run a fever for two or three days around the time of her period, but she did not pay too much attention to this.

"It's nothing. I get this way sometimes. Even though I always go through this sort of thing, it passes eventually, and I get better," she told Kajii.

Though she knew that her health was much better this winter than last, she still spent much of her time in agonizing distress. According to the X ray, she now had two branches on her lung instead of the previous three, and those merely like shadows of pine needles.

"You'll probably always have these," the doctor had said last summer. "It's like a scar after you have a burn. As far as your illness is concerned, you're cured. When the cool weather comes, I don't see any reason why you shouldn't be completely recovered."

Yūko looked forward to the cure he promised, but after autumn passed and winter arrived, her health still would not return to normal. Since her recovery had proceeded at an expected rate up to now, she became quite frustrated. Though she had previously ignored the times when she was not quite up to par, attributing that to the natural effects of her illness, she began to be troubled by the erratic state of her health.

"I still don't feel right. What do you think is wrong?" she would often complain, as if it were the doctor's fault.

"You'll feel strong soon," the doctor said quite calmly. "You don't get over a cold in two or three days under the best of circumstances. And with your history of hemorrhages, do you really expect to get back to normal just like that? Are you continuing to take naps in the afternoons? That's good. As long as you don't neglect that."

She was hardly likely to forget to take those afternoon naps. Her body seemed to wait for the hours between one and three in the afternoon. She didn't go to lie down often because the doctor had told her that fussing overly about herself would delay her recovery. Actually she was at her best for about two hours after she got out of bed in the mornings. From then on, it was a quick downhill slide as far as her strength was concerned. Fatigue began to grip her, stiffness wracked her shoulders and had begun to travel through her neck and into her head recently, so that even before noon she was exhausted. Also, on just the days when for some strange reason she had the idea that she was finally feeling fine, her cheeks would begin to burn up in the late afternoon, and when she took her temperature she saw, to her chagrin, that it registered over thirty-seven degrees centigrade. When Kajii then asked her how she was feeling, all she could say was that there was no change. She simply didn't have the heart anymore to add those encouraging words about how it would all go away soon, as she had in the past.

"I wonder if I shouldn't have gone ahead and had the operation to begin with," Yūko once said thoughtlessly, making it sound like a complaint.

"You're completely wrong about that," Kajii said, frowning.

Yūko had not undergone the operation at the outset of her illness because the hospital had decided against it. However, up until the time the decision had been made, there had been a wide difference of opinion among the doctors. The surgeons had claimed that surgery was the only way to get rid of the diseased area, while the internists disagreed, saying that what with her being over thirty, they could not expect great results from surgery. What's more, since the affected area was shallow and wide, it was better to cure her lung by medicine than by cutting out a huge section. She was also told that losing the full use of one organ through surgery would become a burden on the rest of her body long into the future. But it cannot be said that the wishes of the patient played no part in the choice of the drug therapy method. Although they did not tell the doctors, Kajii was, in particular, opposed to her having a big scar down her back. When they had discussed the advantages of having an operation, he had replied,

"If it's absolutely necessary, then we should go ahead with it."

Then, when he heard the opposing opinions, he had answered,

"That seems right to me. Why, at the office, if three or four of my staff were to leave, the others would become overburdened and they'd collapse. Having people on the staff is preferable, even if they are not as efficient as you would like them to be. I suppose the same thing can be said of the body."

Yūko continued to take the medicine, but once she realized
that after a certain point her body would not return to its original condition, she could not keep her mind away from the operation which they had rejected. If she had had the operation,
she thought, they would have taken out that shadowy pine leaf
configuration on her lung and she would not still feel the lingering traces of her illness. Whenever she brought this up, Kajii
would say,

"If you had had the operation, you might have had to have
another after that to correct the first one and you would still be
in bed recovering now. The worst of this is that you keep dwell-
ing on it. What difference does it make whether your temperature is at thirty-seven degrees or whatever it is? Even people
who have nothing at all wrong with them sometimes have their
temperatures go up in an ordinary day. They just don't take
their temperature every minute, so they don't know what is happening to them, that's all."

One day Yūko was about to take her after-dinner tablet,
but when she drew the tin toward her on the table, Kajii said,

"Why don't you take it later?"

"All right," and she closed the opened lid and was done
with it.

Ever since she had come home, she had put the medicine,
which she previously kept beside her hospital bed, permanently
on the kitchen table. For more than a year, morning and evening, she had been quite conspicuous about showing Kajii the
medicine tin and how she was taking her required dose. Now
she got up and put the tin away in the closet. She felt the blood
rush to her cheeks as she realized what a fool she was to spend
all this time engrossed in her illness, and how a person sick for
so long in this state of mind could become eminently dislikable,
and how Kajii had recently started to get tired of watching her
performance.

She did not achieve the passions of sexual love normally
and sought fiercer modes of arousal, ignoring Kajii's warning,

"This will only make you worse."

"I don't care."

And so, even while he was protesting, Kajii was already exerting more force upon her. For a time, her anxiety had been the goad that markedly increased the sense of reckless abandon. But now she realized that anxiety had become unbearable to him because there had been too many times when she had displayed these inevitable mood changes particular to tuberculosis and refused his sexual demands. When she was actually sick, her debilitation and whining seemed to annoy him. He even appeared to avoid looking at her.

When the overcast, cold weather lingered on for some days, she couldn't go out for walks much. Also, on those particular days, her condition seemed worse than usual which, added to the misery of being stuck in a dreary apartment complex, made her feel she would really lose her mind. She waited impatiently for spring. She was sure that when the warm weather came, her health, physically and emotionally, would improve. But January was not yet over when she felt that she could not wait any longer.

"Why don't you go skiing? Last year and the year before last you didn't go."

Yūko had said this to Kajii, who liked skiing, and had gotten him to go twice. Learning of this, the woman from Takaraya had said,

"Dear me—and leaving the patient at home alone?"

"But I'm the one who suggested it," Yūko said with irritation.

Although the woman was a hard worker and had a good heart, Yūko always discerned a most unpleasant, annoying edge to these uncalled-for remarks. When talk about going away for a cure came up, the woman had said she wished she could afford it herself, which didn't bother Yūko much, but then the woman had to go on and add, with a knowing look on her face,

"But you never know what a man might do if you leave him all by himself." Yūko was so aghast that she could not speak.

Yūko had grown tired of waiting for spring and more and more she longed for the warmth of the Soto-Bōshū seaside. Kajii's company had a health resort where they had gone together when it had already been chilly in Tokyo. As soon as she had set foot on the sandy beach at the seaside, the warmth of the hot earth beneath flowing through her feet, the softness of the air, and the sunlight, which seemed a holdover from late summer, all brought memories suddenly to life with a special vividness. At that time, she had had the impression that the people there were very kind. Once, when waiting at a stop for their bus and trying to confirm where the bus was bound for, they had made inquiries of a young girl in farmworkers' clothes pulling a cart full of vegetables.

"If you wait here, it will come," she had informed them, speaking slowly. But after she had gone ahead a bit, she had stopped her cart and come back to say something else. When they had asked her what she had said, she had told them once more,

"It's ten yen for one person."

Kajii still would not change his opinion about her going away as spring drew closer and closer. But by now there was no connection at all between the season and Yūko's desire to leave. Her longing remained as fierce as ever. Whether they would be strapped for household money, or what Kajii would be up to in her absence did not bother her at all anymore, so great was her frenzy about going to the coast. Could she have convinced herself that her dream was mere whim, she would have been able to relax, but she got it into her head that not being able to leave was impeding her complete recovery. She was simply convinced that if she went, she would be cured. And she told Kajii this over and over.

"Why not just see what happens after two or three months? I'll give her all the medicine that she'll need," the doctor had said. "We'll worry about her getting worse when and if that's necessary. I'll soon make her get well again."

Reluctantly Kajii agreed, though he kept on emphasizing that she would go for only a month.

"A month is just as good as two or three. And I'll be damned if you'll go and fall into a depression. Even now I'm not really in agreement with your going. You're going because you're being so obstinate about it. One month is plenty of time."

The sea around Boso, visible from the train window on this day close to the spring equinox, was bright with a sunshine which seemed warm with spring, but the sea was rather rough. At the seashore, there were not many houses, and low rocks jutted out and the white waves washed across them with a fierce force. The noise reached up to the train window, not only when the waves broke, but also when the waters subsided.

Kajii must have reminded her about the promise to stay for only one month because he now saw the lonely landscape and again felt uneasy about leaving Yūko there. She had nodded.

"A month will be fine."

She meant to imply in her response that no matter how much she liked the place, she would not say that she wished to stay longer than a month. When she finally caught sight of the distant horizon, the near surface of the sea, surging and glinting with sunlight, the small green islets, and the beach which turned dense and shifted color all at once each time the waves receded, she thought that at last she was here at the sea near Boso, which was enough to make strength surge through her.

The room which Kajii had asked the custodian of the company's health resort to find for her was on the second floor of the shop, second over in a brief line of souvenir shops. There were three rooms with a worn reddish tatami covering off the central corridor where the summer bathers must have stayed. A small back room which faced the sea had been selected for her. The man had thought that a big inn would be unsuitable because the food would be the same day after day. While in a small place she would have flexibility in this regard, the old-timers who gathered there to drink would be likely to disturb her with their noise. So he had rented her this kind of accomodation. Yūko had thought that if she could herself locate someone's unused annex, she would be able to do her own cooking but the members of this family (the man was head clerk at an inn and his wife and young daughter ran the shop) prepared her meals.

When Yūko got there, she sensed that her lethargy, the heaviness in the shoulders, the depression and vexations of heart which for so long had been entrenched in her body had melted away in an instant. With each passing day, she felt her body grow stronger. This invigorating potency now expanding within had been denied her for a very long time. There was that same old taste of good health back again. Many times in a day, with nostalgia and pleasure, she affirmed her escape from the world of the sick.

Yūko did not stop taking her afternoon naps, but she was outside most of the morning and, afterwards, until dusk. She went to look at the large fish preserve by the sea, and also to the flower orchard, a bit farther off, and bought bunches of marguerites and stocks at ten yen for three flowers. But most of the time she spent at the seaside. She sat on the deserted terrace of the house by the sea or on the only swing still usable in the row which had been twisted in a previous storm or on a corner of a rock cluster.

The waves looked different each time they broke. Small black coiled shellfish played in the hollows between the rocks. When the water poured through the shelves in the rocks, it sent tattered seaweed surging through and out again. She could watch forever and not get tired. When the sun inclined to the right, behind her, the sea became an absolutely clear dark blue. Having gazed at this for a while, she realized that the wind was starting up and she had to turn back.

Yūko, forbidden to take too many baths in the evening, frequently sat on the balcony and, through the glass partition, caught glimpses of children playing baseball on the beach in the distance. It got so dark that she wondered if they could see the ball without the light, but still they kept on playing until late. They never stopped playing as long as she watched them. But she only had to go away for a moment, then come back, and they had completely disappeared. She never saw them leaving, which struck her as strange. Even eating dinner by herself did not make her feel particularly lonely.

"Will you have some raw sea urchins? Someone brought us

some," the woman of the shop said, offering opened ones with the thorns still on as an addition to the meal. Sometimes the woman would say some such thing and then proceed to stay on and chatter forever. But Yūko did not mind.

Yūko hardly even paid attention to the embroidery, books, and radio she had brought with her. At a bit past eight o'clock, she would feel sleepy, and though she had worried about the noise of the waves, it didn't bother her. At five-thirty in the morning, she would awaken with the freshness of her girlhood.

She was really glad that she had come. She thought she was in paradise. In this new environment, she expected to take a new view of the days when she had annoyed Kajii and had been annoyed by him. She didn't know whether it was because her nerves, usually so on edge, had become duller here, but she could not see any reason to go over that old business again. Sometimes she had a glimmer of those troubles when they came floating into her mind, but the recollections were lightly colored and dim, and since she could not clearly focus upon them, they disappeared. Even her sexual activities seemed like forgotten experiences of a long-finished, old life.

Yūko had days when she suddenly thought that she would start a small souvenir shop or something in the area and try living by herself. She would sell postcards, dolls, candy, real shells (not the manufactured kind), which would be put in net bags, and bunches of seaweed (wrapped up in paper using neither cellophane bags nor labels), which she would sell for fifty or one hundred yen, and wreath shells and dried shells.

When she had come back from a walk, a customer in front of the shop had asked her,

"Hey lady, I want one of these."

And then Yūko had answered, "Thank you very much," and exchanged a package of seaweed for a hundred-yen note.

Although the spring holiday time had arrived and people would be going for trips, there were still not many guests, even on Sundays. The shop women did not spend much time at the front of their shops asking, "How about some souvenirs?" When they had collected a basketful of wreath shells, they would say,

"I'll give you some extra," and would add more from a big box they had at their side. This was their only attempt at commercialism.

If that was the only kind of business acumen required, Yūko thought that even she could master the technique. She felt that if she were to live by the beautiful, peaceful seaside with all the tranquillity, health, and freedom which she craved, then she could go on forever without needing to depend upon anyone.

At about that time, Kajii's younger brother, a teacher, and his wife and son arrived from Tokyo to visit and see how she was getting on.

Before noon, just when Yūko had almost reached her lodging place, out from a clump of bushes by the side of the road at the coast came a voice.

"Auntie!" cried a child, waving his hand. When she looked, she recognized Takeshi.

"Oh, is it you? Who did you come with?"

Yūko went to the edge of the road and spoke down to him below. Takeshi, absorbed in trying to climb through the clumps of grass, ignored her. Pushing aside the grasses which were about as high as he was, and alternately pumping his knee caps up to his chest as he squashed the vegetation, he was trying hard to get to her side as soon as possible. Finally when he did clamber out, he complained, pulling at Yūko's hand,

"Where have you been? We've been waiting for you."

"I'm sorry. Who is with you?"

"My parents are both here," Takeshi answered, still with his hand in hers as he started to walk.

"I'll bet you came on the local express."

"Boso Number One!" Takeshi exclaimed and then quickly added, "I am in the first grade."

When he said this, he looked ahead and, bringing his free hand up to the visor of his brand new official school cap, jerked it slightly left and right.

Yūko, who had intended to say something anyway, now felt that a demand was being made upon her.

"Congratulations on school. You can't wait to go, can

you?" she said, slowing down and bending toward Takeshi, who looked so appealing in his uniform.

Everything about the uniform was done in miniature—the buttons and the grown-up-looking white undercollar peeking over the black collar of his jacket below his tiny chin, the gold buttons lined up in a foreshortened row in the front, and the three of the same style, but smaller, at the square-cut cuffs accentuated quite nicely the masculinity of his round wrists. He might have been diminutive, but everything was there. She was delighted at how odd this seemed. And as emotion flowed through her, Takeshi asked,

"Surprised, aren't you?" and he tried to make her walk faster, pulling her by the hand.

Her brother- and sister-in-law were in her room, seated in front of empty teacups, when they saw her come in with Takeshi.

"You've put on weight, haven't you?"

"You really look well," both of them said.

"That's because I'm being allowed to pamper myself," Yūko responded, and then looked at Takeshi, who had gone to stand by his mother Fumiko's side.

"I'm really glad you came," she said again. "Your student uniform looks wonderful."

Koji looked quite pleased at this and gazed at his son.

Then Fumiko said, "All right, Takeshi, now change your clothes. You have already shown off to your aunt." She pulled her travel case to her side. "Goodness, you've soiled your uniform already!" she cried, getting him to hold up his elbow, which he had apparently soiled when he had rubbed against some dirt while climbing through the underbrush.

His mother pulled him over to the window and dusted him off, but the boy lost no time asking, "When do we eat our lunch?"

Fumiko looked over her shoulder and said, "I don't know whether it's to your taste or not, Yūko, but we brought some for you, too."

Yūko invited them all to have lunch at the seaside. As they went out, the shopkeeper selected wreath shells for them and filled a bottle with soy sauce. She had Takeshi, who was beside himself with excitement, go and gather dried branches from the bushes and pieces of wood deposited by the waves. Near an overhanging rock, she began to build a campfire.

"Yūko, you really know how to do things right," Koji said, taking out a small bottle of whiskey.

"I've always wanted to do this once," Yūko said, smoke skimming past her eyes, "but it's not the sort of thing you do by yourself."

"Is that so? If I were here, I would do it every day."

As the fire started burning, they lined up the wreath shells around it.

"Auntie, do you need more firewood?" Takeshi asked, putting down the four or five pieces of wood he eagerly carried over in his small hands.

"No, that's enough. You've worked hard. Come here and sit by me."

At her side, Yūko spread open another sheet of newspaper, which she held down until Takeshi settled his small bottom on it, the wind having threatened to lift it in the air.

"Look at this shell. Amazing isn't it?" he said, pointing out one in the basket with its lid opened up enough so that he could see the extremely tough flesh of the shellfish inside. He poked a finger at the daunting flesh, but when the shellfish shrank up and closed itself into the cover, Takeshi, alarmed, pulled his hand back and jumped away, making everyone laugh.

For the first time, she didn't take her afternoon nap. Beginning with lunch by the sea, she entertained them all. She was not consciously trying to go out of her way for them. She felt quite exhilarated and not at all feverish. With the others, she took a boat to a small island she had not yet visited, even though it was close by. They examined reef after reef, returned by boat and then went to pick up shells at a different part of the beach. She took pictures and had them taken of herself, simply enjoyed the afternoon and didn't feel a bit tired. Although they were not aware that she usually took an afternoon nap, her brother-in-law and his wife got worried.

"Is it all right for you to be doing this?"

"Shall we go back? If this makes you feel worse, we'll never forgive ourselves," they would say every once in awhile, but even this failed to irk her. She ignored their advice and would move on ahead, demanding of them, visitors there for the first time,

"Isn't this a lovely place? Don't you adore it?"

The sun was going down a bit.

"If you go on like this, you'll wear yourself out. Let the boy go off and amuse himself while we take a rest," said Koji, prevailing over her inclinations. Yūko had sat down with the adults in a small dilapidated boat on the beach, and as she looked over at the sea reflecting the first lights of the setting sun, she said,

"It's absolutely blue. It's always like that at this time."

The three of them sat there watching for a while until finally Koji, without unlacing his fingers which clasped his knees, turned his hands flat and checked his wristwatch. Fumiko also peered over at the watch from the side and said, nodding,

"We'd better go."

"There'll be just enough time for us to go back and pack our things."

"Are you going to take the local express?" Yūko asked, looking over at Takeshi, who was at a distance.

"Yes, that's our plan."

"Why don't you stay for the night?" Yūko ventured.

"That's out of the question. We only came to see how you were feeling. If we stay over and make you fuss over us, my brother will be furious."

"He won't mind. Why don't you stay? You're free with Takeshi's school out."

"But we'll come again soon," Fumiko said, turning down the offer. "Shall we call him?"

Then Koji himself raised his voice to call out, "Takeshi, come along."

Takeshi grabbed the handkerchief he had used for collecting shells from where it sat on the sand. When he stood up, he brought his short arm over his head and, not looking their way, merely waved his palm two or three times as if to say, "I don't want to go."

Even his child's heart understood that this time they were not calling so that they could point out something new to him.

"Poor child, just when he was having such a good time."

Yūko reviewed all the things the child had done in the half day they had been together, starting from his perfectly natural gesture a moment ago. Through the neck of his brick red wool shirt, she could make out the round neckline of his white under-shirt. She recalled how his small body had not stayed still for an instant; how he had come upon a cluster of shells and had jumped about, busily picking each one up; how, when she had found a dried-up, hard-to-find coffer fish (whose name and shape she discovered for the first time since she had come here), which by good chance was in the sand, she had called over to him. Having raced over, he had stared down at the grotesque object and then proclaimed, "I think I'll skip that," putting both his hands behind his back; how he had said to the boatman, who was pulling the oars with all his strength,

"Are we so heavy?"

Now that child had raced even farther off and was bending over.

"He's not coming. You go and get him," Koji said to Fu-miko, who started to get up.

"Why don't you let him stay?" Yūko said, stopping her.

"But we have to make our train."

"No, I mean, why don't I look after him for the next few days." Then she explained, "Two or three days will be good for his health. The day after tomorrow is Saturday and Kajii will be coming. They can go home together the next day."

"But I don't think the boy is up to that yet," Koji said. Fumiko added,

"It'll be too much for you."

Yūko was not to be put off.

"Takeshi, come here," she called directly to the boy. And when she saw him dash away again, she cried out, "I have good news for you."

Takeshi turned around and at last looked her way, then he began to run back to the party. She watched him, thinking that she simply had to persuade him to stay. Her husband would be arriving the day after tomorrow and she would show him her blooming self after two weeks. She could not say that the happy anticipation of a reunion was unqualified. An unyielding depression descended upon her. Kajii had always been quite fond of Takeshi, and so if the boy stayed, she could distract herself with only pleasant activities, like today, and she could end the reunion without incident. The more she thought about this, the more she wanted Takeshi to stay. Now the boy was at her side.

"What is it?" he asked as he dumped the collection in his handkerchief with a clatter on the sand.

"Did you have to go and dump them in the sand? You know you'll just have to pick them up again," Fumiko scolded. Takeshi bent over and rummaged through his small mountain of shells, saying,

"The crab's gone! The crab's gone!"

"Did you say crabs?"

With her forefinger, Yūko poked about among the shells a bit,

"Ran off, didn't it?"

"No, the crab is dead," Takeshi answered, again rummaging through the shells. But only several thin white dessicated crab's legs appeared.

"You mean this? It's all broken off," Yūko said, holding up a leg.

"What should we do?"

"There's nothing you can do. It happened because you put that with the others," Fumiko said, and Koji laughed.

"Takeshi, how about staying on with me?" Yūko asked. "You're a first grader now, so you can manage quite well by yourself, can't you? I'll go and catch some crabs for you. Live ones with red claws. The day after tomorrow your uncle will come and you can go back with him, and take your crabs with you."

Takeshi turned his gaze from the crab's remains to Yūko.

"Where are there crabs?"

"Where? Anywhere!"

"Why didn't you take me there today?"

"I forgot. Let's go tomorrow."

"And my mother and father?" he asked, looking over at them.

"We are going home."

"Will we come here again so I can catch crabs?"

"But I might not be here then," Yūko interrupted.

"What should I do?"

"That's for you to decide."

Then Takeshi said quickly, "All right, you go without me," and waved his hand toward his parents.

But Yūko did not feel secure until the very last moment about whether Takeshi would actually have the courage to remain. At the shop in front of her lodging, she put her hands on Takeshi's shoulders and spoke over his head, winking at her brother- and sister-in-law,

"We'll say good-bye here."

"Sorry to trouble you like this."

"Thank you for lookng after him," they murmured, bowing briefly. They started off and turned to look once more at their son, but whether from a lack of feeling, or from his efforts to hide his nervousness, Takeshi looked down, pulled at the rubber band wrapped around a bunch of seaweed, and made a noise. When she made him turn around in the other direction and escorted him into the house, Yūko finally heaved a sigh of relief.

She didn't feel tired, but since she had walked more than usual, Yūko felt the need of a bath. She nevertheless forced herself to resist that instinct. She asked the landlady to fix the bath only for Takeshi and, from the side of the raised wooden tub, Yūko washed him. When she brought him upstairs, it was already dark outside.

She had him change into the underwear which Fumiko had left, saying that he might get wet playing on the beach. Concerned over the effect that a pitch black sea might have on Takeshi, Yūko quickly pulled the storm windows shut.

"I wonder if I could trouble you for this child's bedding?" Yūko asked, when the daughter of the house came to take out the dinner trays. Even though she had not been infectious for quite some time now, Yūko worried about what the boy's parents would say when they asked later about how they slept. She tucked Takeshi in bed in his undershirt, and Yūko was herself preparing for bed when Takeshi asked her, his head on his pillow,

"Auntie, where are my shells?"

"Don't worry about them," she answered, turning around. "They are safe. I put them all on the railing."

Getting into bed without turning off the light, Yūko surveyed the boy lying next to her. Takeshi was staring at the ceiling and his face, sticking out from under a grown-up's quilt, seemed absolutely small and utterly lonely. What was he thinking about? Was he homesick already? But Takeshi said,

"When are we going to go and catch crabs?"

"Tomorrow."

"I know we're going tomorrow. But can we go as soon as we finish breakfast?"

"Yes, that will be fine."

With that decided, he then said, "Tell me a story," and turned over on his side so that he was facing her.

"You have to pull your pillow toward you."

"All right."

After he had pulled over the rolled-up, towel-wrapped cushion which he had left behind, he put his head on it and again said,

"Tell me a story."

"A story, a story. What shall I tell you?" she said, stammering slightly. Since she had no experience with telling stories to children, she didn't recall the beginning of the two or three stories she did remember or know the best way to relate them.

"Well, Takeshi, why don't you tell me a story instead," she said, searching for a way out. "Even a television story. Which do you like—General Ponpon?"

"No."

"Well, what will it be?"

"I don't like television."

Then Takeshi jerked his body around again on the bed, and, lying almost flat on his stomach, put his hands to the side of the pillow.

"Scratch my back," he said. Yūko emerged from her covers and inserted her hand under the collar and down the boy's warm back. Moving her bent fingers around, she asked,

"Where does it itch? Here?"

His face pushed down into the pillow, Takeshi nodded imperceptibly.

"When did it happen? Maybe a bug bit you?"

"I always have my back scratched when I go to sleep," he said. "A little bit higher . . ."

While Yūko did as he instructed, Takeshi closed his eyes in apparent enjoyment, but as she continued, he complained,

"Don't always scratch the same place."

As he made demands for this or that spot, she realized, astonished, that he never ran out of new areas on that small back. Yūko would move her crooked fingers to the right and then to the left, insert them farther down the boy's back and then work up, scratching in short strokes, that resilient young flesh under the shirt. She was constricted further by the weight of the heavy quilt. Her hand got a bit tired.

"Go back to where you were before," he said and Yūko again moved her hand. "A little lower. Lower than that."

"You mean here?"

"No."

Although his eyes were closed, his eyebrows registered irritation. "No, not there, lower, towards my stomach."

With a wry smile on her face, Yūko immediately started to scratch at the side of his chest. But soon Takeshi's imperative utterances gradually became faint, more distant, and finally inaudible. His breathing deepened. He was really still a baby, she thought and, gazing at Takeshi's innocent sleeping face with its slightly protruding lower lip, she again set him in the center of the pallet.

Under her own blankets and dropping her head on the pillow, she noticed that she had forgotten to turn off the ceiling light. She was about to throw off her blankets and get up when her eyes caught sight of Takeshi's student uniform hanging in the wardrobe. The small outfit was on the hanger, front open and golden buttons reflecting off the yellow light. The two little arms, caught in the hanger, stood straight out and took a haughty attitude in their elevated position. For a while, she stared openly at the uniform from her pillow.

Lobsters were being raised in the shallow wooden tub. They had all straightened themselves out and sunk down to the bottom of the water as if they were stuck there. Occasionally, they thrashed unexpectedly. What Yūko was showing Takeshi as they squatted down and peered into the tub was not the lobsters, but the small sea turtle which had joined their ranks. As they had passed by the shop, three men were looking into the tub and were saying,

"Unusual." "You rarely see anything like that."

And Yūko, along with Takeshi, had gone over to see what they were talking about.

"The sea turtle. It was just born yesterday," one of the men explained. In color and shape, the turtle was fully formed, but the shell measured only three centimeters in diameter. The turtle swam slowly to the left and to the right, close to the water's surface. There were no toes on the four legs, which were still all skin.

"Will this grow big?" Yūko asked. "Big enough for people to ride it?"

"Yes."

She addressed Takeshi, who was gripping the edge of the tub with both hands, looking at it.

"That Urashima from the fairy tale, his turtle was like this. When this one grows big, people will be able to ride it. The legs are webfooted, aren't they?"

Takeshi was silent as he nodded. The turtle made a paddling motion on the water as if it were beginning to use its legs one by one. Each time, perhaps because it did not know quite how to swim yet, the turtle veered this way and that.

"I wonder if you'd care to sell it to us?" she asked.

"It would die right away. Only people who live in this coast town know how to bring these things up."

"But I'd be happy to have it for just a while."

"We're actually just taking care of it for someone."

She would not have believed that one small turtle, no matter how unusual, could be so precious to the local people, the area being what it was.

"Oh, I see. I didn't understand," she apologized for her disrespect. She regretted her own stupidity in even trying to negotiate for the turtle in the first place and thus perhaps making Takeshi feel bad about leaving it behind.

"Well, thank you then," she said to the men. "Come along, Takeshi," she had signaled him, uncertain whether or not he would obey her. Fortunately, he followed without any fuss.

After a while, he asked, "Where will we go to find the crabs?"

The whole morning had passed without her finding him any crabs. When she had seen the baby turtle swimming at a tilt a few minutes ago, she had instantly made up her mind to buy it—she thought the owner would be glad to sell it to her—and had calculated with a sense of relief that she could use it as compensation in case they could not find any crabs. Takeshi now might have had some inkling about the unexpected difficulties involved in finding crabs. Maybe a baby turtle would make him forget about the crabs, or so she thought. But from what Takeshi had said just now, it seemed that even if they had been able to acquire the baby turtle, he was by no means ready to forget about the crabs. What Takeshi believed was that she could help him find a live crab which waved bright red claws and ran clattering in sideway hops.

"Takeshi, it's noon, let's go back and have lunch and then take a nap."

"Nap? I don't want to take a nap."

"You must. If you take a nap, you'll grow big. Even crabs take naps. If you go looking for them at nap time, you won't find any."

This plan had been in Yūko's mind from the outset. Upon

awakening, she had not felt any worse for all the extra walking she had done yesterday, and in fact her body had become accustomed to it, but she was most reluctant to break with her long-standing habit two days in a row. Especially with Takeshi here and Kajii coming tomorrow, if she felt in any way out of sorts, there would be problems. After lunch, Yūko finally persuaded Takeshi to take a nap. Alternately pulling up and kicking off the blanket, he asked,

"What time can I get up?"

"Three o'clock. I'll tell you when, so don't worry about it."

Takeshi tried to close his eyes tight, but soon opened them again.

"Auntie, do crabs sleep stomach up like we do?"

"What do you think, Takeshi?"

"I don't know."

"I don't think I know either. Be quiet now and go to sleep," she said, closing her eyes.

"Auntie, I think they sleep with their stomachs up."

Pretending that she hadn't heard, Yūko remained silent. Takeshi did not seem to need to have his back scratched for his afternoon naps. When she looked over at him after he had become quiet, she saw that he was already asleep. Yūko closed her eyes again.

Although she called it an afternoon nap, all she actually did was lie down and close her eyes. She almost never slept. When she had first started taking naps, she had been troubled by the tendency to let her mind dwell on her problems, but eventually she developed the habit of being able to fall into a state closely approximating sleep even while she felt the light strike her eyelids.

But today was different. As soon as her afternoon nap was over, she knew that she would have to go out and look for the crabs again. She was longing to find some for the boy and so was not able to relax, so anxious was she for three o'clock to come.

"Do you know where there are any crabs?"

Since morning, Yūko had asked this question numerous

times, first to her landlady. "You see, the boy would like some crabs."

"There are some around here," the landlady had answered. "Where the waves come in on the beach."

"In the sandy part?"

"I think so. When we gather clams at low tide, we see a lot of them."

Remembering that the dried-out dismembered crab which Takeshi had found yesterday had been in the sandy part, Yūko took Takeshi with her and set out for that area.

With the sunlight pouring down on them, they tramped along the wet strand. Here, no dead cats or bits of radish or even a single torn sandal came floating up. The seaside was beautiful. All of the footprints dotting the shore belonged to them.

"I'm going to try and dig for some," Takeshi said, stuffing into Yūko's bag the nylon sack that he had snatched up when they had left the inn, for use in case they caught any crabs. Spreading his legs and cupping both his hands, he began digging out the sand toward himself.

"Wait a minute," she said, stopping him and unbuttoning his shirt cuffs. Clasping each of his wrists by turn, Yūko felt as if she were peeling each of his thin, short arms as she rolled both the sleeves of his shirt and undershirt up over his elbows.

Takeshi set about his work with great enthusiasm. The sea water seeped into the bottom of the sand pit he had made.

"Looks like there aren't any here," Yūko said, standing and looking down.

"I'll dig in another spot."

But no matter how many times he dug, the only thing that came up was sea water.

"Auntie, maybe there are some further upland away from the beach," he said, running over to the dry end of the beach, which he surveyed extensively.

Still finding no crabs, Yūko beckoned to Takeshi and, allowing him to pick up a few more shells, they walked toward the highway. They headed beyond the station toward the fish preserve created out of the natural reef. The people who ran the preserve were wholesalers of fish products. The diving women's boats were pulling into port and going out to sea in the area, casting nets were hung out to dry, and the smell of brine was especially heavy. The place raised Yūko's hopes although she did not know why. When they approached the fish preserve that morning it was deserted.

"I'll ask over there," Yūko said to Takeshi and went to make inquiries at the shedlike house built on the reef behind the preserve. When Yūko opened the rattling wooden door, she stared at the dirt floor of the dim interior and the coarse baskets piled up to the ceiling. After calling out, she saw an old woman emerge.

"I wonder if you could tell me if there are any crabs?" she asked without preliminaries.

"You mean sand crabs," the old woman nodded, making a circle to indicate their size with her hands and saying, "They're not very tasty. We can't catch many. We don't carry them."

"No, not the crabs you eat, I mean the small ones . . ."

"Oh, the ones you keep as pets? The ones with red claws?"

"Yes, those," Takeshi answered.

The old woman narrowed her eyes and looked at the child, "Oh, it's those you want? Where would you find them now? You won't find many crabs around here. But how about looking at some fish in our preserve?"

"Shall we have her show them to us?" Yūko asked Takeshi.

"Preserve? What does that mean?"

"There's a big hole below this place which the sea water fills and they raise fish there. They have abalone in baskets and other fish. What would you like to do?"

"Makes no difference to me," Takeshi answered.

"Then shall we leave? Thank you very much anyway," Yūko said and they started to go out.

"Where do you think the crabs are?" Takeshi asked.

Three middle school students, their arms on each others' shoulders, came toward them on the other side of the street.

"Those boys must know," she said to Takeshi, and called out to them just as they were going to pass.

"Do you boys know where we can find some crabs—the small kind you keep as pets?"

"What did you say?"

Arms still around each other, they came across the street and Yūko repeated the question.

"Is that what she wants?" the students asked, looking at each other. "There must be a lot of crabs around." They smiled vaguely, ready to leave.

"Where are they?" Yūko almost pleaded.

Still in a group, they moved ahead at an angle, looking back over their shoulders, while the boy at the far end told her, "We don't know."

Watching the students go off, Yūko couldn't tell whether they were shy, or really didn't know, or were just teasing her.

"Why didn't they just tell us where the crabs were? They said there were some," Takeshi asked resentfully.

"They probably didn't know. I'll ask someone else," Yūko consoled him.

As she started walking along, Yūko was reminded by those students about the middle school up ahead on this road which those young boys must be attending. The school was on the high ground across the highway from the beach. From the spacious grounds, the view of the sea was superb. Two or three times during her walks, she had, without permission, used the bathroom in the corner of the school ground and each time she had thought that teaching at the school might be pleasant. The teachers there probably commuted to work by bicycle and went fishing on Sundays. A biology teacher there might possibly use his extra time for research on the different kinds of fish in the area. Such a person would immediately be able to tell them very knowledgeably about where the crabs lived around here. But now it was spring vacation, and that was impossible.

A young girl carrying an empty basket emerged from the clumps of vegetation along the seaward side. She had probably been drying seaweed on the beach. Taking Takeshi's hand, Yūko approached her and asked again whether there were any crabs in the area.

"You find those in the mountains," she answered.

"In the mountains?" Yūko fairly shouted. "Not in the sea?"

"The ones with red claws, you mean?"

"Yes."

"Red crabs. They're called fresh water crabs because they're found in the mountain springs. Children tie strings around them and play with them."

"Those are the ones I mean. There are no crabs around here?"

"Small ones like specks of dust are all you'll find here."

"What color are they?"

"They don't have any color. If you pick up a stone along the coast, they'll come running out."

If there were so many around here, then at least one must be big, even though it had no color.

"Thank you," she answered.

But when she thought about the matter further, she realized that there were not that many places around the shore where there were rocks one could not only budge but also find crabs sheltering under. There were either stretches of sand or massive reefs, or if not these, then shoals deeply planted in sand and washed by the waves.

With Takeshi in hand, Yūko made her way to the beach along various paths—through a grassy passage that seemed easy to clamber down, a road with an arrow pointing in the direction of a large inn, and a lane between private homes with tall television antennas stuck on their roofs. The situation was as she had feared.

"This place is hopeless too. There are no such rocks here," she had to tell Takeshi each time.

"Which place was she talking about, I wonder," Takeshi pondered as they turned back.

At long last, Yūko discovered a place on the coast with stones as the girl had described. Several rocks the size of footballs lay scattered on a sandy stretch where the tide did not come in except during a storm. This was far from being a place where crabs would likely be found, but Yūko, who had wanted to give Takeshi at least the opportunity to move some rocks about, took him down to the spot.

"We're lucky," she said.

"I'll move the stones. If any come out, Auntie, will you grab them for me?"

"All right."

They must not let any crabs escape once he lifted a stone, so they had to proceed cautiously. Takeshi, his hands gripping the rock he had set his heart on, began to lift it up bit by bit, all the while peering under it until he was almost standing on his head. Yūko faced him straight on, and their heads almost touched. She stared in at the space under the stone.

"See any? Auntie? Are there any crabs there?" Takeshi asked excitedly.

Despite their difficulties finding crabs, despite their numerous failures, the boy showed no sign of giving up, even though he did keep asking "Why can't we find any?" or "Where did the girl mean we could find some?" He would always add, "When will you find me some?" "Where will we look now?"

Was his preoccupation with the crabs they couldn't find growing stronger, or was he merely demonstrating the innocent cruelty of a child who believed that adults could do anything? Yūko could not bring herself to say that he should give up when Takeshi spoke like this to her. On the contrary, unthinkingly, her replies increased his eagerness. Now she yearned for that moment when she would grab a crab which, its claw at the ready, was scuttling away sideways. She would tell Takeshi, "I'm catching it for you because if you got your finger caught in his pincer, it would hurt," and drop it into the transparent nylon bag.

"Not yet, Auntie?" he asked again.

"Not yet. Try lifting it up a bit more."

As she peered into the depths of the crevice, her head cocked and bent almost to her feet, she so longed to see the crimson claw brandished by the crab in alarm at the sudden sunlight invading its domain that she felt the muscles between her brows grow stiff.

Takeshi had not yet awakened from his afternoon nap. Yūko closed her eyes once again.

Really, why weren't there any crabs? If only she had been able to get the man to sell the baby turtle to her. But Yūko knew that even if she had, she herself could never relinquish the idea of capturing a crab so long as Takeshi did not say that now that he had a turtle, he no longer needed a crab.

When she had promised him yesterday that she would find him some crabs, she had not resorted to guile in order to persuade him to stay. She felt that somewhere in this whole wide coast at least one crab would come running over if she would call out to it. Hadn't that been true for all the people she had come across thus far? Everyone who had given her advice had perhaps sensed that there were crabs around and had spoken of the places where they thought they had seen them. Just like the landlady who had said, when they had returned empty-handed,

"Is that so? You didn't find any? I have the feeling that I saw some when I went shell gathering at low tide. But it's still a few days before the first of April and the open season. When I saw the crabs, it must have been later than this."

She had gone on in that vein. In that case, Yūko realized that the junior high school students may have been the most admirable in answering "We don't know" to the question "Well, exactly where are they?" after they had declared, "There must be crabs all over."

Were there, in the final analysis, no crabs to be found here? They still hadn't had a look at the reef ledge by the coast, but perhaps that was no good either. The girl may have been right—maybe fresh mountain springs were the only places where they could be found.

Yūko suddenly remembered that occasionally some narrow fields in the region had the earth retained by stone walls. True, it wasn't in the mountains, nor were there freshets, but the impression she had was that there had been some wet patches of ground. She'd been searching in the wrong places; maybe she would find red crabs there. Getting up, she decided that she would go and have a look while the boy was still asleep.

"Are you going out?" asked the daughter of the house, who was right below her as she went down the stairs. She didn't think the girl would understand her abnormal concern about crabs and so she felt shy about telling her bluntly where she was going.

"The boy is sleeping. Would you just keep an eye on him? I'll be right back," Yūko answered.

She put on sandals and went out onto the dirt floor. The landlady, who was squatting on the ground just then with a middle-aged man, a bucket between them, turned around to Yūko and said,

"I'll prepare sea urchins again for you tonight."

Wet sea urchins, their brown shade close to black, were in the bucket, their round ball-like bodies, consisting only of spines, moving imperceptibly. The man took them out of the bucket and put them on the ground. After he had taken them out, they could see the other things he had caught. They were the size of ping-pong balls and had green hair all over, seemingly packed in tight way down to the bottom.

"What are those?" Yūko asked.

The man replied, "Those are also sea urchins, but you can't eat them. I catch them and use them to make dolls."

Yūko, who had never seen where sea urchins live, asked,

"What kind of place do they live in?"

"On the beach where there are lots of stones. I pick up those stones one by one."

"Are there crabs there?"

"There are all kinds—there are hermit crabs and starfish also."

"So if you remove the stones, you'll find crabs?"

"Yes. They scatter in a comical way."

In other words, what the girl had told her about lifting rocks, Yūko realized, had been in reference to this type of rock along the beach.

"Are there only small ones? Or are there any this size?" she said, using her forefingers to describe a matchbox size.

"Sometimes you see them."

"What do you mean, sometimes?"

"I mean there aren't enough of them so that they'd scatter. Today there were about ten of them."

"With red claws?"

"No, around here, they don't have red claws. They're the same color as the back."

They'd have to settle for crabs which didn't have red claws.

"Where is this place you were talking about?"

The man mentioned the name of a coastal area less than an hour's train ride away, from where boats plied to Uraga.

"Is the beach close to the station?"

"About twelve or thirteen minutes, I'd say. It's on the opposite side from where the boats dock," the man informed her.

"Do you think you'll go?" the landlady asked from the side.

"I don't know. Depending upon what happens, we may go tomorrow or so . . ." Yūko replied. She had already decided not to investigate the stone walls around the fields. Tomorrow Kajii was due to arrive around evening, and so during the morning, she thought she'd take Takeshi and go to the beach in question. However, judging from her experience until noon, she had no choice but to approach the project with caution. The object in question was a living organism. Even if there had been ten today, there might not be a single one tomorrow. Also, perhaps it might rain and they might not be able to go. And the day after tomorrow it could still be raining. She decided not to tell Takeshi yet. It was clear that if she didn't tell him, she must simulate supervising the search until evening.

It was a bit past three P.M. and Takeshi was still asleep. Since she had promised to tell him when the time was up, she woke him. Then she got some sweets from the store and had him carry them. Together they went to the reef ledge along the coast.

The tide had begun to come in, but still, here and there along the reef, were sunken hollows of water. Pointing out those spots, Yūko said,

"Takeshi, maybe there are crabs here." She indicated a linear fissure in a huge boulder.

"Keep your eye on it. They may come out soon."

Yūko now knew another spot with greater possibilities. For this reason she must have lost her enthusiasm for the place she now surveyed. Takeshi seemed to sense this. They had not found

any crabs and Takeshi had been picking up small black rolled
shells from the puddles for a while. Standing up, he held both
his hands around the transparent nylon bag containing his
catch. Then he came over to Yūko, who had sat down on the
reef.

"Why don't we go back. There aren't any crabs," he said.

And then, a seeming result of Yūko's indifference and her
untrustworthy behavior since morning, he added, as if he had
given up on her,

"When Uncle comes tomorrow, I'll have him catch some
for me."

"Takeshi! How could you say such a thing!" she exclaimed
in a voice so outraged that Takeshi's eyelashes twitched. Her
face became red, and not only from jealousy.

"Takeshi, don't you dare say such a thing."

Yūko caught herself and started to speak more gently to the
boy, who had bowed his small head,

"Be a good boy and don't tell Uncle when he comes about
how you want to find crabs. And don't tell him about our coming today to look for them and how we couldn't find them."

The moment Yūko realized that Kajii might find out about
how much she had been obsessed with finding crabs for Takeshi,
she became so ashamed that she flushed. This was beyond Takeshi's understanding, but he must have been cowed by her threatening attitude a moment ago. Takeshi didn't ask her the reason
he couldn't tell his uncle anything. He nodded, looking down.

"If we don't find any crabs by the time you have to return
home, the next time you come, I'll find you some. I'll ask about a
place where there are some."

"But I might not come again."

"Then when I go back to Tokyo, I'll bring you some."

"All right," he murmured, feeling a little better. "One
thing," he said, and finally raised his head.

"What is it?" she asked, putting her hand on his shoulder.

"Can I tell Uncle about the small turtle we saw swimming
around?"

After appearing to think a bit, she answered, "I don't mind
that at all."

"What about my telling him that we made a campfire and ate fresh wreath shells?"

"I don't mind that at all."

"That we went to the island by boat?"

"I don't mind that at all."

"That I found a crab yesterday?"

Reflecting only momentarily on the question, Yūko replied, "I don't mind."

But what about Takeshi's plan to go to the beach tomorrow? She had already begun to ponder the matter. She would be more than willing to take him to the spot if Takeshi spoke to Kajii only about the crab Takeshi had picked up.

Happiness

by Uno Chiyo

UNO CHIYO (1897–   ) attained prominence in the Japanese literary world for her stories about the complications of love. Much of her writing is based upon her own hectic romantic entanglements, but the elegant, quiet style distinguishes her work from melodrama. As the characters in her stories pursue the objects of their affections despite rejection, social censure, and murderous weather, Uno follows them on every reckless rendezvous to offer perceptive psychological analyses.

Some critics consider the novella *Amorous Confessions* (*Irozange*, 1935) Uno's most representative creation. It is based upon the experiences of the painter Tōgō Seiji, with whom she lived. The hero spends his days trying to tidy up his cluttered private life, but the queue of women is relentless in demands upon his energy and time. In another novella, *Ohan* (1957; trans. 1961), the hero, in a less modern setting, similarly fails to free himself from emotional chaos. It might be said that for Uno Chiyo there are no love stories, only the desperate search for gentleness in a life which refuses to yield meaning.

Uno's heroine in "Happiness" (*Kōfuku*, 1970) can speak with satisfaction of her independence from the world of men after decades of futile questing. This story won the Women's Literature Award.

1.

Every time Kazue gets out of the bath, she stands in front of the mirror and examines her naked body for a moment. She uses the towel in front for modesty and turns her hips slightly, standing at an angle. Her skin has turned slightly pink.

"I look like her," she thinks.

She thus notes her resemblance to Botticelli's Venus. There is the similarity in the way that she is standing although no sea shell supports her. She also has the same feet and slightly rounded stomach. This description might imply that Kazue enjoys staring at herself at length, but in fact this is not the case. She just notes the resemblance and soon gets dressed.

In fact, Kazue does not very deeply believe that her naked body resembles Venus. A body with more than seventy years of wear behind it is hardly likely to come close to Venus's. Perhaps Kazue's skin bears blemishes in places and occasionally sags. But her eyesight is failing and the steam from the bath makes the objects before her even more obscure. Kazue includes these shortcomings when she enumerates the happy aspects of her life. In this manner, Kazue collects fragments of happiness one after another, and so lives, spreading them throughout her environment. Even what seems odd to other people, she considers happiness.

Five years ago, Kazue separated from her husband and at that time she wanted to make it painless. Kazue herself came to think of the separation as all for the best, and so when her husband had gone about his packing, she had been of some service to him, which she considered perfectly natural.

Her husband had left her to live with a younger woman. Although Kazue never saw the woman, her husband had known her for quite a while, and so she had a pretty good idea of what kind of woman she was. Kazue was hardly surprised that her husband would leave her to live with that woman. Kazue lived with her husband for a long time, about thirty years. When you live with someone for such a lengthy period, you start to ignore the other person, almost as if the other person were not there. Not only did she think her husband lived by himself, but Kazue also sometimes thought of herself as living alone. Without giving consideration to her husband's preferences, she sometimes quite calmly went about doing what she wanted.

During the time when the two of them were living together, Kazue was constantly at her husband's beck and call and did only those things which would make him happy—or so it seemed. This appeared to please her, but closer scrutiny reveals that Kazue did what she wanted without considering the other person's wishes at all. She always approached matters from her own point of view and unconsciously selected only those activities which pleased her or which she thought interesting or fun. She did things which gave her husband pleasure because she herself found them interesting. She did things others found pleasing when she herself would be amused. She took pleasure in thinking about things from her own point of view and, looking back upon these matters, she realized the selfish pleasures she had derived.

There was that time during the war when they had evacuated to Atami and, since their house was close to the town, heard rumors about possible bombings. Although making a target of such a small hot springs resort seemed unlikely, rumors were then extremely common everywhere. Just about the time they were contemplating a move to a more remote area, someone told them about a country home on a small mountaintop not far from Atami built by a person of unusual tastes. The house had no running water, and so it was necessary either to collect the rainwater or go down to the river in the gorge and haul it back. If such conditions were agreeable, they were told that they could rent the place.

In her youth, Kazue had lived in a mountain cottage where she had gone down to the river in the gorge to bring back the water supply. Far from finding this chore troublesome, she recalled the pleasure she had taken in the work. After she told this to her husband, they both went for an inspection and found that the mountain was not as high as they had anticipated. The sliding doors and the roof were visible through the spaces between the trees at the top. The house gave the appearance of proximity and also seemed quite far up.

"Do you really think we can live in such a place?" her husband had asked her in astonishment. "And do you really think we'll be able to go down into the valley and bring back the water?"

"Why, I'll go and get the water," Kazue had replied.

Although she thought that the inconvenience could be borne for the sake of living in a safe location, her husband did not share these sentiments.

Even now, Kazue remembers those days. At the outset, she probably had every intention of pleasing the others, but as matters developed, she had at times gone forward thoughtlessly, and done things they did not like. She remembers bristling with resentment at having given up a project—this despite the warning from others that she was being disagreeable.

Once Kazue decides upon a plan, she soon finds herself absolutely taken up in the enjoyment of seeing it through. Perhaps living in that house on the mountain and bringing water up from the river down in the gorge might have proved interesting temporarily, but after a long period would have been bothersome. Although her husband had no doubt that this would be the outcome, if he had not been so outspoken in opposition, they probably would have moved into the house. Now even Kazue can laugh at her peculiarity.

Undertakings which Kazue can arrange alone, without consulting others, she throws herself into absolutely, without a backward thought. Instead of moving to the house on the mountaintop, they moved from Atami to the country home of her husband's family in Tochigi. After having shipped their belongings by train, her husband went on ahead by himself to the countryside, while Kazue remained behind to pack up the smaller items. Fearing that the sesame oil they had bought on the black market might, if shipped openly, be confiscated, Kazue wrapped the oil can in a large cloth and took the train from

Atami, carrying the bundle on her back. At that time, with the war nearly over, the train had no roof and the passengers were packed together like canned sardines. It was near Shinagawa Station where talk of air raids circulated and the train stopped. With bombings a real possibility, she wondered why the crew didn't make a dash for it, but the train paused and they could hear the sound of the bombs falling. The train itself escaped damage.

Later, she realized how fortunate she had been that the train had not been bombed. Without a roof, the train was an easy target. She had the oil on her back and so, had the train sustained a bomb attack, the flames would have engulfed her whole body. Not only Kazue herself, but the other people in the train, packed together like sardines, would have become victims of the fire. Kazue never thinks quite that far ahead when she embarks upon a project. All she knew was that she wished to make food cooked in her oil for the people who had evacuated to the country, and that once she produced the food fried in the oil, she would be able to watch the enjoyment fill their faces. This was as far as she had considered the matter.

Even at the country place in Tochigi, Kazue made the rounds of the farmhouses in order to collect food to eat. Strangely enough, Kazue was quite skillful at finding them provisions, a task she also found absorbing. Like everyone else, she exchanged the Japanese and Western clothes in her possession for food. Often, however, she would walk along with a heavy pack on her back and come upon a small-scale air raid in progress. With barracks close by, the one or two enemy planes would swoop down a mere ten meters from the ground, so close that she could see the faces of the American pilots inside.

"Ah, there's one walking along. Maybe we should shoot her," they seemed to be saying to each other in jest. Strangely enough, Kazue did not feel afraid at those times. Why wasn't she afraid? She did not know why. Perhaps she had convinced herself that those men would definitely not attack her in such circumstances.

In the country, Kazue worked hard. Even though she had

usually slept late in the mornings, she got up before her in-laws. Which was odd. Perhaps her husband's parents had done her the favor of waiting in their beds until she got up. She lit the fire on the hearth and made the morning soup. In the garden, not yet completely daylight, a mist still hovered. Kazue made the meal with the foodstuffs she had herself collected. She made good meals and her in-laws and husband praised her cooking skills. She thoroughly enjoyed this work and, as it turns out, she does not recall the wartime as having been an especially difficult period. Looking back, she thinks of the fun she had.

To have fun. That is the theme of Kazue's life.

2.

Kazue always tries not to think of herself as an unhappy woman, and even though most people think she is unhappy, Kazue does not think so herself. Why is that? She does not quite understand the reason, but perhaps it is because she is more of a coward than most. It frightens her, the pain of thinking herself unhappy, and so she determines to consider herself happy, which has become her daily habit.

One morning, when the war was just beginning, an order came conscripting her husband for the Azabu regiment. In such a circumstance, what was left for Kazue to do? She did not know where her husband would be sent. Perhaps he would just go away forever at this point. Although she was not permitted to see him, Kazue would bring food boxes and fruit baskets to the regiment. Whether her husband received these items, she did not know. In any case, she brought the food to him. What should she bring? How could she get it to him? That was all she needed to think about. Later, she found out that none of the food had reached her husband and all that remained was a story, laughingly related, about a woman who came daily with packets of food. Looking back upon that now, she does not think that she had wasted the food, for merely carrying the things over had been compensation enough for her.

On a snowy morning, her husband set out for Java. Kazue

and her father-in-law were not certain which day he would leave. Having only heard a rumor that this would be the day, they stood in front of the regiment, just as the dawn was breaking, while many soldiers emerged from the gate in khaki clothes that did not look like army uniforms. Perhaps one was her husband? They were supposed to take the train from Shinagawa, and since some time would remain before the departure, perhaps they would be permitted to see each other then. Kazue and her father-in-law walked with the soldiers on the snowy streets, though they had no idea what the distance was from Azabu to Shinagawa. The sun had begun to shine on the snow. Her father-in-law was past seventy (approximately Kazue's age now), but he said nothing about being tired. There was the smell of the soldiers' clothing and their perspiration, and, although she felt certain that her husband was among them, she had not located him by the time they finally reached Shinagawa. Many soldiers had collected in the garden of a large house, actually a mansion unfamiliar to her. Was her husband there? The station platform looked intimidating. There was paper strewn all about. When the wind rose, the scraps of paper flew everywhere. She wanted to go down to that platform, but as she stood looking down from the upper deck of the station, quite unexpectedly, someone she knew came out of the crowd.

"Did you see him?" she was asked.

Just five minutes ago, she was told, her husband's unit had gone off on the train. Before leaving, her husband had raised a black-gloved hand in greeting to this acquaintance. Kazue had bought her husband those gloves when he had gone off and he must have felt sorry, thinking of Kazue and his family whom he had not been able to meet. But Kazue did not feel regret when she thought that if only she had come five minutes earlier, she would have been able to meet her husband. She had walked all this distance and had not been able to meet him, but she did not regret it.

"Father, let's go home."

"All right."

The two of them took a taxi home.

Kazue lived the next year without her husband. It is difficult to wait for someone whose return is uncertain. This was the sort of life that was perhaps most trying for Kazue. Kazue could not maintain her own spirit in the abstract and continue with nothing changing around her. At first she had stuck a calendar on the wall and crossed off one day after another. How long would she have to keep this up? She did not know. She wanted to fix some goal about how long she would have to continue this waiting, but even that was not possible. She could not continue in such a routine, with no definite limit in sight. One day (she can't remember exactly when) Kazue simply removed the calendar from the wall.

More precisely stated, could it be that Kazue relied only on what she saw with her eyes and derived pleasure only from acting solely on the basis of this evidence? At that time, Kazue quite often went to visit a dollmaker in Awa and in her letters to her husband she would write, "I went to Awa again," enclosing photos of the dolls which that artisan had made.

She had heard that her husband was not actually in a combat zone. Even so, her letters were gauche, considering the fact that they went to one thousands of miles from home who had no idea when he would be returning; but she had thought her correspondence appropriate until her husband came home later and told her, "All those letters about dolls were irritating."

Perhaps Kazue ceased to understand the differences between her own sensibility and that of the person far away. Or does she err just because he is far away? Did she think that the only way to cheer him was to move his heart with matters that she herself appreciated? As her husband's stay in that distant place grew longer and longer, she lost her ability to visualize the elements of their relationship. Indeed, she stopped being able to visualize her husband's physical appearance and he seemed likely to disappear entirely.

Even Kazue herself does not understand the independent projects she undertook during this period. She could not visualize what her husband looked like and so it was difficult for Kazue to capture her husband in the abstract. Naturally, Kazue had possessed the very same normal feelings toward a husband who had been shipped off that afflicted any other woman in the world. But at some point, she seemed to lose sight of these emotions and, moreover, Kazue herself was not aware of this.

Before she knew it, in each of the letters Kazue wrote to her husband, she utterly forgot that he was far away and that the time of his return was unknown, and she wrote only about herself. Was it a misunderstanding on her part, her belief that her husband would take pleasure in this? She sent the pictures she had taken of the rearrangement of the furniture. This and the other domestic changes became so extensive that her husband would not believe it was the same house he had left. Did she want to surprise him with how the house had changed? In any case, Kazue did not just sit and wait for her husband, but did something positive even though that might just possibly annoy him.

"This spring I planted peas in the back garden," she wrote, sending a picture of her picking them in the pea field.

What did Kazue do after she had sown the peas? To write about those things is difficult. When her husband did return, Kazue cannot forget that mixed in with the pleasure that had welled up in her at his homecoming was a confusion which made her feel as if an alien creature, cut off from everything else, had suddenly appeared in her midst. This was due to the dismay her husband showed as he looked dazedly at the sweeping changes in the house.

3.

Kazue often deviates from the normal way men and women generally live together. Where she begins to deviate, she does not know. At any time, she might set her mind on something and chase after it, and with these activities, the process begins. Had the person with her known beforehand that she was about to start doing something, he would have put a halt to everything; but to protest while she was in the middle of something was too late, for Kazue would have already committed herself totally, and by that time, stopping would have been most difficult.

Most men ended up watching Kazue's activities at this point. It was unlikely that they could have asked Kazue, "Why don't you consult with me before you start on something?" By the time they realized what was happening, Kazue had already started. Her actions were like a gust of wind—gone before you knew it.

Although it is impossible to believe, Kazue has built eleven houses from her youth until today. One day she itemized the lot on her fingers and counted a full ten houses that she had already built. And now she is in the process of building the eleventh. There must be people in this world who long to build only one house of their own during their lifetime. And there are people who have not built even that one house. What has impelled her to build eleven houses one after the other? Perhaps Kazue is just that avaricious?

Looking back now, there are houses among that eleven so primitive as to be hardly considered houses at all. And then again there are luxurious houses upon which she spent a small fortune. And there are houses she had built for some reason or other and did not even live in for a month. Once when the seasons changed and she went in to check, there were bamboo shoots growing between the straw mats. If Kazue's avariciousness is not in any way the problem, perhaps something more important is lacking? Kazue was not very shocked at the sight of bamboo shoots growing out from between the straw mats, nor was she saddened when a house upon which she had thrown a small fortune was repossessed because she could not keep up the payments.

When the moving van came—Kazue can't recall having turned around to look at the house with regret as she left it for the last time. It was not even a matter of regret because she already did not think of that place as her home. Strangely enough, Kazue had already formed an attachment to the small, shaded house that she was moving into. In that small place, perhaps she would set floor lamps with paper covers. In the normal course of events, Kazue naturally should be hurt by such happenings, but by acting positively, she quickly passes through that bleak stage.

She has to act positively, this was always necessary, but Kazue did not act positively just because it was necessary. Before she herself even realized it, she had already acted. And this, in every instance, insured that Kazue would not be hurt. Always, everywhere, Kazue is not hurt. Is that possible? Upon deeper consideration, Kazue has never just done nothing, never stayed in the same place for long just because she has gotten hurt.

Possibly others think that Kazue is like the lizard who still crawls around without knowing that its tail has been cut off. Even though she has lost her house and moved to the place in Aoyama, she never compares the two residences because the present one is the house she will live in from now on. In a manner of speaking, she thinks of the former house as a mere shell. From the very day she moves, she is attached to that shaded house. It is not a matter of whether she feels a clean break is best. It is just that she is in a hurry to reach her destination, and destinations are the only things that Kazue gets excited about.

What is a destination? She does not know. For Kazue, is there something at the destination resembling happiness? Is happiness not the accumulation of the present circumstances upon which one builds, or, rather, is happiness something that lies ahead after she gets through her present circumstances? Is the surging ahead the only thing for Kazue? Is she merely going forward restlessly without even being conscious of the something ahead? Is it mere animal strenth? Kazue does not know.

"You don't need a back gate on this house," Kazue's sister laughed. "You'll be able to crawl in and out through the hole."

She mentioned this because the concrete wall still had a large hole left over from the ravages of war. Kazue did not even notice the hole.

4.

When Kazue moved to the house in Aoyama, she had thought first about how her husband would best be able to do his work. There was an annex to the Aoyama house. And there was a slightly better room there, where her husband could quite peacefully go about his activities. And so Kazue and her husband went back and forth between the two wings. There were times when he was busy that her husband shut himself in the annex. When Kazue undertook a project, she sometimes forgot to inform her husband about it. There were times, afterwards, when she would let the matter of telling him slide. Unconsciously, Kazue and her husband lived two separate lives. Kazue went over to the annex occasionally, to show off the beautiful kimono she was working on.

"Very pretty. The color combination is pretty," her husband would say. Her husband's calm expression was that of a neighbor, for when he said that Kazue's work was beautiful, it was indeed the opinion of a neighbor, as far as he was concerned. Kazue does not ask for more than this measure of involvement and so this sort of communication became a habit. They lived together in that place, where they excluded all emotional influences, avoiding all contact. Or they put on the appearance of not seeing while actually seeing what the other person was doing, and in this manner they minimized the injuries they inflicted upon each other. Injury? That was true. Hadn't many of Kazue's rash actions inflicted injury upon others when they came close to her? It was, however, at about this time that Kazue finally realized that in the context of her married existence, she was the one inflicting injury. And only recently, when all those events had disappeared beyond the distant clouds, has she come to understand this.

Now, after having gone through various adventures, Kazue has again set upon building her eleventh house. Since she built her first house, this is the third time she has built a house on this mountain site. Building three houses on the same land? She is not now living with anyone, and so as soon as she has an idea, she can implement it the very next day because she does not have to worry about talking to that person and having him tell her to stop doing such and such. At first she definitely would begin with the feeling of wanting the person she was with to like what she was doing, but somewhere along the line, she would veer from this course. At some point, Kazue's feelings simply drive her to do exactly what she wants. And when that happens, it is the same thing as not having anyone with her which sometimes is at the source of her foolish behavior.

Kazue cannot ignore her feeling of stranded isolation. The last person she was with separated from Kazue at this point and observes what she does from the sidelines. None of her men follow wherever Kazue goes, but see her off from behind. Hadn't Kazue gone through exactly the same process each time she married, and wasn't it at that point that the relationship had come apart?

Kazue is now on the second floor of her eleventh house. She can see the withered forests and the mountains off in the distance through the glass door. The snow is falling. It is mountain snow, so different from the snow which descends onto the city sidewalks. Light and powdery, the snow falls steadily, silently. The snow has collected on all the trees' withered branches, but nonetheless a faint light has come shining through. On the way over to the house she noticed that the snow drifts break off abruptly and ice was spreading across the stream there. In this snow, the house still has a bit more work to be done on it. Actually, she will pass the winter with the construction incomplete.

"Here she is, way past seventy, and building a house," people are said to criticize her. "It's crazy."

Perhaps at this age, not building a house is a more reasonable way to live—is this what is meant? But Kazue has already built her house. The white snow on the mountain ridge can be seen hazily in the distance. For a moment, Kazue's heart is taken up with this artificial world where prudence is thrown to the wind. It is the endless stretch of white snow which transports Kazue into that world.

At the height of winter in the mountains, the heater in the room is sometimes totally iced over since the outer walls are not complete.

"Nasuyama is cold, isn't it?" says the red-cheeked boy with a rising inflection as he comes in to fix the heater.

He probably means to imply that spending the winter on

this cold mountain is too much for her. Although the water pipes freeze and frequently there is no water, Kazue does not think of giving up her winter hibernation. Perhaps this is a measure of Kazue's arrogance? Isn't this the same attitude she had taken about being able to live in that house on top of the hill in Atami during the war? She has just not calculated how much effort it would take to ameliorate the various inconveniences and simply thinks that acting positively will be sufficient.

But Kazue is now alone in this mountain house. Perhaps because no one tries to stop Kazue from acting positively, she does not have to think about hesitating because the other person objects. Her only restraint is lack of money, and there are perhaps times when she does not even pay attention to this. Kazue probably does not feel the loneliness of living by herself since, as was mentioned before, Kazue collects any number of fragmented bits of happiness from her existence and lives with them at her side. For there is the great enjoyment she experienced the moment she looked down from her second-floor terrace and saw that the stream had frozen over and the water had formed small mirrors of ice. Is this her way of protecting herself? But there is also the fact that Kazue can recall the turmoil which welled up in her heart on the day she wondered whether all the men she had lived with were on the sidelines observing her and, standing at the spot from where they had sent her on her way alone, had heaved a sigh of relief.

After separating from Kazue, all her men married other women. As if they had for the first time reached their destination, all the men would relax peacefully in their married life. Kazue was aware that even outsiders noticed this fact. It could be said of Kazue that she came to the conclusion that her men had begun to lead normal lives after they had left her. Was Kazue jealous of them? She does not think so. The peaceful lives of the men she had broken with seems to Kazue predictable.

The snow does not stop. Perhaps two feet have accumulated. On the side of the house, there is a road which becomes a gentle slope. She cheerfully imagines how perfect this spot would be if she knew how to ski. Since the snow started falling yesterday, all tire marks have vanished from the road. The house is surrounded on all four sides by the same thick growth of scrub, and the thin branches of the trees with their load of snow look, from every angle, like lace. The sun is still out and the snowflakes are dancing upwards. The winds have risen.

A Note on the Translator

Phyllis Birnbaum was educated at Barnard College and Berkeley and is the author of the novel *An Eastern Tradition*, based on the years she lived in India. Her essays, translations, and book reviews have appeared in numerous publications in the U.S., India, Japan, and the United Kingdom. Work on the translations published in this volume was supported by a grant from the Translation Center at Columbia University.